A DISCARDED PEARL

.

A DISCARDED PEARL

A MARSDEN ROMANCE BOOK FIVE

DAWN BROWER

MONARCHAL GLENN PRESS

CONTENTS

For everyone waiting to finally find out what happened to Damian and Pearla. It wasn't too long of a wait, just a little longer than I planned. I hope their story lives up to your expectations.

CHAPTER ONE

*H*eat filled her cheeks as she rushed across the dock toward the ship she'd secured passage on. Pearla Montgomery wanted as much distance between her and England as she could possibly get. Had anyone ever experienced such monumental embarrassment?

"No. That honor only goes to me," she muttered under her breath.

She had been so close to marrying Noah St. John, the Duke of Huntly. She'd fallen in love with him the moment she saw him. The hurt spilling out of his chocolate brown eyes...all she wanted to do was wrap him up in her arms and ease the pain away. Noah didn't or, to be more accurate, *couldn't* love her. She knew that, but she hoped in time he would at least come to care for her.

Unfortunately, his not-so-dead wife had crashed their wedding. *Had it only been that morning?* Rubina had waltzed into the church without a by-your-leave. Not that the woman needed permission. Her husband had been about to marry another woman. In her position, Pearla would have done the same. If only she'd come home sooner and prevented the resulting embarrassment. For that alone, Pearla resented her intrusion.

No one had known Rubina lived. Noah believed he lost her to a watery gave when a ship she'd been sailing on capsized in a storm. Pearla believed if he'd been aware Rubina was alive he'd have searched for her. The duke hadn't said much about his wife, but it was clear he loved her. The tone in his voice changed whenever he said her name. When she'd appeared at the church, it had become clear the duchess's resurrection was the end of Pearla's relationship with Noah. It was a combination of sadness and happiness that filled her heart at the sight of Rubina. She was ecstatic for him, and morose that she had to relinquish the connection they'd shared. Rubina was the woman he loved; Pearla was the usurper in their relationship.

"Just my luck." Pearla sighed and marched toward the ship.

She'd rushed home, demanded her maid to remove her wedding attire, and ordered her trunks packed for a different trip. If she never laid eyes on the bloody dress ever again, it'd be too soon. At the day's start, she'd thought she would be moving into Noah's townhouse. The staff had been given instructions to send the trunks to his home later in the day. Pearla was no longer going to be his duchess, and never would be. Not that she wanted the title; it'd been the man she craved. Sadly, she had to let go of that desire. Now, here she was, hours later, preparing to embark on an alternate excursion. The sun would be setting on all her hopes and dreams in a few hours. This was a day she'd not soon forget, but not for the reasons she originally thought.

"Can I help you, missy?"

Pearla turned and held in a breath. She cringed at the sight of the burly man before her. His demeanor was menacing, and he was covered in dirt and grime. By the smell of him he'd not deigned to bathe in several days—perhaps weeks. He stood near the gangway to board the ship, blocking her path. She lifted her chin and glared at him as haughtily as she could manage.

"I am Miss Pearla Montgomery. I have passage on this ship."

"Do you now?" His eyes leered across her bosom. "Why don't you wait here while I go and find the Captain."

It took everything she had to not visibly shake under his lewd gaze. This was just a means to an end. It wouldn't do to stay in England and watch Noah being blissfully happy with his wife. No one expected Pearla to stay and witness their reunion. Her best friend, Gemma Marsden supported her decision. She was happy for Noah. Truly, she was.

However, she wasn't in the least joyful at her own circumstances. Running away from the problems life had thrown at her wasn't an ideal situation. Everything she'd done since her wedding had ended in failure screamed of desperation. It was a sad fact. She'd loved a man who wasn't available. If only she'd known before she'd suffered the shame of loving him. Losing him and what they could have had… She shook her head and cleared her thoughts. Noah wasn't hers. That unfortunate outcome was for the best. Marriage hadn't been in her plans until he waltzed into her life. It was time to do what she'd originally intended. Travel the world and see what it had to offer. The morning's disaster prompted what should have been her path all along.

"Miss Montgomery?"

Pearla's gaze shot upward and landed on a tall man with a scruffy beard. "Yes."

"My bosun tells me you've secured passage aboard my ship."

She played with her lip between her teeth. There better not be some mistake. It would be awful if she'd been played a fool and some thief, under the guise of booking her passage, stole her funds. She had to be on this ship. "I spoke to someone named Paolo about an hour ago."

He narrowed his eyes and studied her. He nodded. "I am Captain Blythe. I do recall Paolo saying we would have a couple passengers. Please, follow me."

A couple of passengers? She didn't bring a lady's maid. The idea of having anyone with her...made her uneasy. It was not something she wanted to deal with. As far as she was concerned, she didn't have a reputation to salvage. Why put up with someone that would only get in her way. Still, she couldn't help wondering who else was supposed to board the ship. She hoped the captain didn't expect them to share a cabin. Pearla wanted to be alone, and having a cabin mate would be too annoying.

The captain led her below deck to a small room with one narrow bunk. She breathed a sigh of relief. With only one bunk, surely that meant she would be alone as she wished.

"Do you have trunks that needed to be brought aboard the ship?"

The captain's words snapped her out of her own mind. "Yes. They are in my carriage. Do you have someone that can retrieve them? If not, I can have the footmen bring them aboard."

He nodded. "I will have my men secure them below deck."

Pearla set her valise and reticule on the bunk. The only things she expected to have on the long journey were inside her traveling bags. The rest she'd worry over later. She didn't even have any idea where this particular ship was heading. It had the only thing she required when looking for passage: it left immediately.

"Captain," the burly man from earlier interrupted. "Our other passenger has arrived."

The captain turned toward him and said, "Perfect. Then we can set sail as soon as the anchor is hoisted."

The man stared lewdly at Pearla. She gulped back unease that pooled at the bottom of her stomach. She would lock her door after they left. The way the man looked at her made her skin crawl.

"Are you wishing me to keep you company?" The disgusting man licked his lips suggestively. Pearla lifted her hand and held a finger under her nose. The captain needed to control his men better. This one in particular needed to understand his place better.

Pearla shook her head and stumbled back into the room. "No. I'm fine. Honestly. Perhaps you should help with the new passenger." She gestured toward the captain.

"Leave the young lady alone, Perry," the captain ordered. "She's right. I do need your help with our new guest. Besides, the boss gave express instructions to make sure we keep Miss Montgomery safe on her journey."

Perry? She wrinkled her nose. Even his name was distasteful. The captain's smile made her feel even more uneasy. Paolo must be his boss. He did seem overly concerned for her welfare. Maybe she had lucked out in that regard. She certainly hoped so because she didn't like how Perry was ogling her. He smacked his lips as if anticipating his favorite sweet treat would touch his tongue. It wasn't something she particularly liked seeing. He was a combination of scary and disgusting. Did he believe in bathing at all? She wanted to cover her nose and mouth again. It took every ounce of etiquette instilled in her to refrain from doing so. He could leave the cabin and his offending odor would still linger.

"Too bad. We could have had some fun, you and I." He wiggled his eyebrows. "Let me know if you be changing your mind."

"While I appreciate your, um…" She paused, considered her words, "offer, I must decline."

"We will leave you to make yourself comfortable." The captain turned to leave. "Please stay in your cabin for now. You will be in the way as we set sail. I will let you know when it's safe to come on deck."

Pearla nodded. She didn't have a problem with the request. She was more than happy to wallow in self pity in her cabin. It would give her time to properly grieve what she lost. The man of her dreams… How does a woman get over that?

The captain closed the door with a *click*. A key turned in the lock. *What the hell?* She said she would stay in the cabin. Why would the captain lock her inside? She walked over to the door and yanked at the door knob, hoping she'd been wrong. Unfortunately, she wasn't. The damned man had made it impossible for her to leave.

That uneasy feeling turned into angry knots pounding through her whole body. Her breathing became frantic. There was very little light in the cabin. The small porthole only allowed a tiny stream of sunlight into the room. Was she to suffer in the dark? She scanned the room to see if perhaps there was a lantern she could light. Nothing.

She stormed back to the door and pounded on it with her fists. "Let me out. Let me out now. I can't breathe."

No one came to her rescue. She was truly stuck. What had she gotten herself into?

Pearla crumpled against the wall underneath the porthole. Letting the sun bathe her in what little light the hole allowed. She let her face drop into her palms as tears fell from her eyes. In everything that happened, she hadn't allowed herself the time to cry. She'd lost so much, and apparently she was about to lose much more before the day was done. It served her right for acting so foolhardy.

Stupid. Stupid. Stupid.

Pearla wasn't sure how much time passed as she gave into her misery, but it seemed like ages. She glanced at the porthole. There was still some

DAWN BROWER

sunlight, so night hadn't fallen yet. When she arrived on the dock it had been early evening. The setting sun gave her something to work with time-wise. With the onset of warm weather, they gained more daylight hours, which meant she'd been locked in the cabin at least a couple hours. The door creaked open, and Pearla shot to her feet. Finally, someone was coming to let her out. They had heard her. *Thank God.*

A body was shoved inside. Whoever it was tumbled to the ground with a loud *thud.* Just as fast as the door opened, it was closed again. She hopped over the unconscious figure and pounded on the door.

"You can't leave him in here with me. Come back," she shouted. "There isn't room enough for one person, let alone two."

They ignored her. Bloody rotten bastards, the lot of them. She would get even with them for being so inconsiderate. Her fists clenched tight against her side as her cheeks flushed with heat. It might take time, but they would regret treating her like common baggage.

A small groan filled the silence. Perhaps she should check on her cabin mate. Who knows what they did to the poor soul. Pearla kneeled down beside him and rolled him over onto his back. Sunlight spilled across his face, and she sucked in a breath. He had an angry knot swelling across his forehead, but everything else about him was perfect. Inky black hair curled around his shoulder, and his face was almost too pretty to be considered handsome. She brushed back his hair to get a better look at his injuries. He moaned with her ministrations. His eyes flew open and she once again had the breath knocked out of her. His eyes were so beautiful. They were a silver gray that sparkled in the tiny sliver of sunlight sliding through the porthole.

"Who are you?" His voice reminded her of warmed brandy. She'd only consumed the amber liquor once; it'd been enough to know she'd been playing with fire. When this man spoke, his rich timber was similar to that blaze engulfing her from the inside out.

"I should be asking you the same. Why would Captain Blythe toss you in a cabin with me and lock the door?" Pearla shook her head. "What did you do to anger him?"

More importantly what had she done to deserve such ill treatment? At least they didn't shove a malodorous beast into the cabin with her. She'd not have been able to suffer through such torture.

Perry's stench had been rotten. This man almost smelled—nice. If she was forced to share her space with a disreputable man, she could be thankful he wasn't disgusting to gaze upon either. There could be worse fates...

"I had the audacity to disagree with his boss's treatment of my sister." His eyes narrowed. "What did you do to anger him?"

She chewed on her bottom lip. "I don't have any idea."

"What is your name?" he asked.

She shook her head. "You first."

He chuckled and then winced with pain. His hand flew to his forehead. "Fair enough. But have pity on me. I have one bloody hell of a headache."

A smile twitched on her face. "I reserve the right to make life as difficult as possible, sir. I do not know you."

"I think I like you." A cocky grin filled his face. "I am Damian Leone or Conte Leone if you prefer formality." He lifted his hand and traced his fingers across her cheek. "If I get a choice, I'd have you call me Damian."

She raised an eyebrow. "Just Damian?"

"Yes. I have a feeling you and I are going to be spending a lot of time together."

Pearla frowned. "I hope not."

"Does my company displease you that much?"

How was she to explain it had nothing to do with him. This whole mess was not his fault at all. He was quite charming and beautiful to behold. She would have been entranced with him under other circumstances.

"You don't figure into my consideration. I am not familiar with you enough to ascertain if you're likeable or not." She shrugged. "However, I do have to find a way out of this cabin."

"I hate to tell you," he paused and sat up. "But we are not obtaining our freedom for some time. The ship is already sailing out of the harbor."

Pearla cursed and stood. She headed to the porthole and looked outside. The blasted man was right. They were already well on their way. How long had she been in the cabin before they tossed him inside with her? It didn't matter. They were stuck together. She'd have to make the best of it.

"Come, *cara,* and tell me how you found yourself in the company of such disreputable ruffians as those in the employ of Paolo, the Duca d'Sordillo."

"Who?" Pearla sat down on the bunk and huffed out a breath. "I'm not familiar with that name."

"No?" Damian frowned. "That doesn't make

sense. Why would they stick you with me? Tell me your story; maybe I can figure it out once I have all the information. Why are you on this ship?"

"It's kind of a long story." How to explain her failed wedding to a stranger? It wasn't something Pearla looked forward to. She didn't even want to think about it let alone put voice to it.

"I have nothing but time, *cara*." He waved his hand toward the porthole. "I think it's accurate to assume we will be confined to each other's company for the foreseeable future."

"Quit saying that," she demanded.

"What?" he asked, confused.

"I am not your darling."

"Ah." His lips tilted into one of his half-cocky smiles. "You have yet to tell me your name. What else am I to call you?"

Why did he have to have a valid point? More importantly, why did she still refuse to tell him her name? Maybe it was the fantasy of it. There was a certain romanticism to it all. Instead of telling him her name, she told him her story. This was exactly what she needed upon further reflection. A stranger was much easier to talk to then friends. Gemma had meant well, but she could see the pity mixed with concern in her friend's eyes.

"Today was supposed to be my wedding day," she began. When she finished, a loud whistle filled the room, and then he cursed more colorfully than she had.

"Bloody hell, you're Miss Pearla Montgomery." He scrubbed his hands over his face. "It all makes sense now."

"Well, I'm glad you understand what is going on." She crossed her arms across her chest and glared at him. "I sure don't. I'm as confused as ever." Like how the hell did he know who she was? She hadn't mentioned names. All she told him was her fiancé's presumed dead wife interrupted her wedding. The desire to leave England had made her jump on the first ship available. Had rumors spread that fast already?

His next words made her heart almost stop.

"Rubina is my sister."

She had the worst luck of anyone alive. Only she would have the misfortune of being stuck in a room with the brother of the woman who'd ruined her life. Someone out there truly hated her.

CHAPTER TWO

"*I*gnoring me isn't going to solve all of your problems." Damian stared at Pearla. The sun was low in the sky, illuminating her golden blonde hair. He could see why Noah had been attracted to the beauty. She'd been bloody obstinate for weeks. They'd managed small talk when it was required. Nothing personal or what they needed to discuss. She was pouting because he'd tried once again to broach the subject. "We *are* going to be stuck with each other for a while, so we might as well get to know each other.

When Rubina showed up at his ship near Palermo, he'd been overjoyed to find out she was alive. After he'd gotten over his shock he couldn't stop hugging her. They rushed back to England to stop her husband's wedding. Not once on their race to get there had they stopped to think how it would affect Noah's fiancée. It saddened him that his sister's happiness caused Pearla misery. When she'd told him her story, he wanted to hug her for different reasons. The lost and lonely look in her eyes called out to him. He wanted to erase all of her worries and make the world a better place for her. She was a headstrong woman though and refused to talk to him. How was he to ease her concerns if she wouldn't share them?

If he was correct, Paolo had brought them together for a reason. Whatever nefarious scheme the evil man hatched could be their undoing. Paolo hated him, but hated Noah more. Pearla had been set to marry the duke. Hurting her only meant one thing: it was a way to get even with Noah for obtaining Rubina's love. He'd gone over every detail in depth, and there was no other reason for Paolo to kidnap Pearla.

"I'd rather not." She leaned against the cabin wall and folded her arms across her generous bosom. "If it's all the same to you, please pretend I'm not here."

Damian chuckled. Stubborn chit. "Let's talk this over a bit."

She turned toward him, her eyes a blue flame

sparkling in the light. "I already told you I don't want to speak to you. Why are you being so relentless?"

She needed him. Why couldn't she see that? Damian would get through to her. He'd never been able to resist a woman in distress. Pearla put on a good show, but he recognized the fear she tried to suppress. He made her uncomfortable. It was up to him to put her at ease. She didn't realize how fortunate she was to have him locked in the cabin with her. Any other man would have taken advantage of the situation. Honor prevented him from preying on innocents.

"Because we are in a bind, and you may not like it, but you and I are in this mess together."

They'd been on the ship for days—no weeks. Damian had no idea how long she stewed in silence. She even ate their meager meals without complaint. What woman could hold back their disdain with such ease? Their captors didn't make life easy for them. Each day had begun to blur into the next. It had to have been at least a fortnight, probably longer. It was time for her to stop being so bloody stubborn. They'd no doubt be reaching their destination soon.

"When we reach port, I will find a way out of this

cabin and put as much distance between us as possible." She lifted her hand and ran her fingers through her mess of curls. She cursed as they got stuck in a knot. They'd not been allowed baths, but they'd been provided with a pitcher of water, a small basin, and a bar of soap. Pearla had used the water and soap to wash her face and hair. He'd offered to help her, but she'd refused. Her hair dried into the mess of curls she fought to run her hands through.

"Do you have a brush in your reticule?" he asked.

Earlier, her eyes had been pure fire—the gaze she now threw him was pure ice. How she could go from one emotion to the next, Damian didn't know, but he wanted to find out.

"Why do you ask?"

When would she give in and stop being so difficult? He'd let her use most of the water for bathing. He'd only had enough for a quick wash. Surely she'd start to see, at some point, he wasn't a bad person and could be trusted. Damian sighed. "I can brush out the knots if you'll let me."

Pearla stared at him as if he'd grown three heads. Was it so odd for him to offer to help her? He wanted to make her as comfortable as possible. Noah had cared about her, and if something happened to his former fiancée he'd blame himself.

His sister finally had her husband back. They didn't need any unnecessary guilt from whatever Paolo had in store for them. He was a devious bastard and was capable of anything. Besides, Damian rather liked her. She appealed to him. The little details she did impart only wetted his appetite for more. Miss Montgomery was willful, brave, and full of surprises. All traits he found intriguing, and it didn't hurt she was gorgeous.

"I don't think that's a good idea."

Damian shrugged. "Suit yourself."

He wasn't going to force her to allow him to help. There would come a time he would need her to trust him. When they did reach a port, they would have to rely on each other to escape. If he pushed now, she'd be less likely to follow him to their own mutual safety. In the short time they'd been locked in the cabin together, she'd come to mean something to him. When given the opportunity he'd like to explore what was between them. Their situation was complicated and wrought with emotional overload.

Pearla dug through her reticule and pulled out a brush with a polished silver handle. With a sigh she picked up the brush and tried to run it through her golden strands. A bit of sunlight hit the handle of her brush and blinded him. Damian cursed and shielded his eyes. He couldn't watch her with the sun daring to get in his way. *Blasted sunlight.* He wasn't lost on the irony. He craved to be outside enjoying the sun's warmth, but it was preventing him from enjoying the only lovely view available to him.

Pearla winced. Damian couldn't stand watching her torture herself. "When are you going to give in and let me help you?"

He wanted to know if her hair was a silky soft as it looked. But he also wanted to help her, and she was refusing something so simple. He could brush her luscious locks better since he had easier access to the long tresses. They were so long that they fell past her waist in waves.

Damian clenched his fists at his side. These were not thoughts he should entertain. He needed the lady to trust him. It would do no good for her to know exactly how much he desired her. If she'd allow it.

No, he wouldn't go there. She was not for him. His life was far too dangerous for a wife and children. He couldn't risk a family when they'd only be at constant risk.

Another wince filled the room. Bloody hell, when would she give in? He thought Rubina was stubborn —Pearla took it to all new levels.

"Fine." She threw the brush at him. "See if you can do a better job."

"Why, *cara*, you beg so sweetly." The corner of his mouth twitched. He fought the smile that wanted to form. "Since you asked so eloquently…"

Finally, permission to touch her. Yes, it was to brush her hair, but it was something he craved. One concession would lead to another, and before long he'd have everything he desired. He wanted to be deep in all she had to offer. One taste or one touch would not be enough. All he knew for certain was that she was the one woman he desired more than any other. Maybe it was because he believed her to be forbidden.

She glared at him. "Don't make this even more difficult than it already is."

He winced as he stood and walked over to her. Pain shot through his side with each movement. Paolo's men had done a number on him. He'd begun to heal, but it would still take several more days for him to be at full strength.

"Turn your face away from me." He sat down on the bed beside her. "I will be able to get the knots untangled better with full access to your lovely hair."

"Quit trying to be charming. I am immune to the

likes of you." She threw the words at him as she turned her body.

Damian wanted to see if she was as immune as she claimed to be. He doubted it. Noah had told him that he was only marrying Pearla so he could have children. The Duke of Huntly needed heirs. His brother-in-law believed he was incapable of loving any woman other than his sister, Rubina. Seeing his former fiancée in the flesh, he found it hard to believe he wouldn't have fallen in love with her eventually. Hell, he was half in love with her already, and he'd only been in her company for a short time. He shook his head. What was this nonsense he was thinking? He didn't love her. Lust? Definitely. Love was an entirely different thing.

"Your hair is as silky as I thought it would be." He picked up a few strands and ran the brush through them. "You shouldn't have let them get so tangled. We could have avoided this if you had tried to brush it hours ago."

"Forgive me for having more pressing matters on my mind," she spat out. "My hair was the last thing I thought to take care of."

Damian chuckled quietly. It wouldn't do for her to know how her anger amused him. "Rightly so. This is a precarious situation we are in."

She sighed. "Tell me why they put us together."

"Why are you suddenly interested in your fate?" He raised an eyebrow. "You seemed perfectly content to ignore my existence for days now."

He couldn't help needling her. It was about bloody time she started to get on board with what was happening to them. She needed to know everything if she was going to be fully armed for the battle they were going to face. They'd wasted too much time with her stubbornness. He'd tried to tell her what happened with his sister several times. Paolo was an evil man and his deeds shouldn't be taken lightly. They were on the ship together for a reason. Damian hadn't ascertained what that was yet, but he had a feeling they'd find out soon. Whatever the duca's plans were, Damian was sure of one thing— they wouldn't end well. His sister's tale was one of torture, both emotional and physical. He wanted to spare Pearla such a fate if possible. Their own predicament already bordered on it.

"I wasn't ready to admit I needed to know. When Rubina…" She paused and took a deep breath. "It was more than I could deal with. I had to get away. You wouldn't understand."

"So you loved him?" Damian asked softly. He cursed inwardly. Of course she did. From what he understood, many women had coveted the title of Duchess of Huntly. It would have taken someone extra special to catch Noah's eye. The duke had standards. He wouldn't have chosen Pearla lightly, especially since she would've been the mother of his future heirs. So he'd wooed her without giving her his heart—Pearla apparently hadn't been so lucky.

Damian hadn't begrudged Noah any happiness. His sister loved him, and for that he'd wanted to see him happy. It'd been clear to him that Noah hadn't been without her. The duke went through the motions, put on a good show, but the sadness never left him. When Noah believed Rubina died, a part of him had too. It was something Damian could appreciate, in a way. He loved his sister, but romantic love was something he'd never experienced. He had no idea how he'd react if he'd lost the love of his life. If he ever experienced such pain, he hoped he could live through it with as much grace as his brother-in-law. How Noah managed to survive it, he would never understand.

"I thought I did. Maybe I was in love with the idea of love." She turned her head slightly. A tiny tear fell from the corner of her eyes. "I had plans. I wanted to heal his heart. Oh, I know he didn't love me... But I thought, in time, he'd at least come to care for me. It's taken me the days I've spent in this cabin with you to come to terms with what I've lost."

Damian paused, holding the brush against her hair. He could understand that a little bit. It wasn't easy to lose a dream. Noah wasn't the love of her life, but that didn't make the plans she'd made any less important. He resumed brushing and inhaled her scent—a whisper of lilies mingled with vanilla.

"I suppose we should start at the beginning." Damian needed a distraction and talking was the best one he could come up with. "Paolo is obsessed with my sister. She didn't leave Noah willingly. He held her captive and arranged for everyone to believe she died." Rubina's supposed death had nearly destroyed Damian, and he'd thrown himself into his work with the government to bury his grief.

Pearla gasped and jerked around to look at him. "That's terrible. How did she manage to get away from him?"

"It was pure luck." He sighed. "We've been watching Paolo for different reasons. He's an evil man and has ties to the Sicilian mafia. We don't know how deep he's in…"

"So you rescued her?"

He shook his head. "No, my man Arturo did. He discovered her presence by accident. He'd been working undercover as their gardener. When Paolo left for business one night, Arturo brought Rubina to me."

Damian hadn't believed it was her at first. He wanted to, but the shock of it... Anger at the unnecessary grief came crashing down on him all at once. Paolo had to pay for the injury he caused his family. Rubina came first. They left Palermo immediately to see to her care. On the journey to Naples, they made plans and discovered Noah was in danger. He still was if Rubina hadn't eradicated the problem. His only choice was to have faith in his sister, and her husband. Noah wouldn't stay in the dark for long. He'd made his suspicions clear when he came to Damian's room to collect Rubina. That had been one of the longest days of Damian's life. Noah and Pearla's failed wedding day would be forever ingrained in his memory. Now, he was stuck on a ship and couldn't help his sister. All he could do was pray she was able to eradicate Paolo and keep her husband safe. He had a new objective; Pearla's safety was his utmost concern.

"That must have been quite a shock for you. I remember the look on Noah's face when she showed up to the wedding... Everyone else disappeared for him. I knew then that he never would have loved me, at least not the way he loved her." Her voice was tinged with sadness. It broke as she spoke. "It hurt to see it."

He found himself wanting to console her. No one should have their heart broken in such a manner. It was too late to prevent it, but maybe he could ease her pain in other ways. Loving a man shouldn't be a hardship. It should be a joy to be reveled in. Noah unwittingly destroyed a part of her. The reason for it didn't matter. The fact it happened was all that counted.

"You deserve to have that kind of love. Don't sell yourself short."

"You're right. I needed time and distance to see that for myself." She turned her head slightly; a tiny wistful smile filled her face. "Are you almost done brushing my hair?"

Damian stared at her lips. He wanted to kiss her. The desire flooded him to his depths and he fought for control. "Almost, *cara.*"

"When are you going to cease calling me that?"

"Never," he replied.

"I wish you would. That is a lover's term." She frowned. "We are not lovers."

Not yet anyway... Damian had no doubt they would be someday. It was no longer a matter of if, but a matter of when. Something about her made him want things he shouldn't. This might not end well. Perhaps he should give into his desires and take what they both wanted. He wasn't ignorant to the little looks she kept throwing him. She had a bit of desire growing inside her too.

Instead, he finished his story. "To make a long story short we knew Paolo was in England. We were hoping to find him before he did something to Noah or my sister. It looks like we were too late. There is no better way to hurt both of them than to kidnap us both."

Pearla gasped. "But, I don't mean that much to Noah. That's ridiculous."

"You keep telling yourself that if it makes you feel better. He may not have been in love with you, but Noah did care about you."

Damian was glad his sister was alive for more reasons than one. It freed Pearla to find someone who would appreciate her. Noah cared for her, but not enough. He'd never have gotten over his sister. Pearla was better off, and soon she'd realize it.

Her mouth fell open at his words. "I…"

"It's all right to accept that you meant something to him. You were going to be married after all."

Damian was rather glad that wedding didn't

actually happen. The lust flowing through his blood wouldn't have boded well with his relationship with Noah. The man would have killed him if he'd touched his wife. Lucky for him, she was unencumbered and he could let his desires run free.

"You're right. You're damn near perfect. Why wouldn't you be?" She bit her lip. "Of course you are. It's a lot to let sink in. What does this mean for us?"

Paolo was determined to make him pay. It wasn't only because the duca was obsessed with his sister. He had other reasons for hating Damian. Pearla was caught up in a mess he'd made. If he could change things… He shook his head. The time for regrets had passed. He owned his mistakes, and it was time to explain his part in the mess they were in.

"I've never claimed to be perfect." He lifted his hand and ran his fingertips over the top of her head. "Mistakes are a part of life, and I've made my fair share of them."

"Do tell." She goaded him. "What was the one mistake you regret the most?"

Believing his sister had died. No, that wasn't his mistake. It was something someone forced upon him. "I seduced a woman for information. It didn't sit well with me, but I believed at the time the end justified the means. I was wrong, and it hurt her terribly."

Paolo's sister had been that woman. She'd been innocent of any wrong doing. She'd been forever altered from that transgression. He'd broken her heart after he deserted her. Damian couldn't change what he'd done, but from that moment on he'd vowed to never do anything so malicious ever again.

"You used a woman and you expect me to have faith in you?"

He had to be honest with her. Telling her had been a risk, but he'd hoped she would see it as him being open. Damian didn't want to hide anything from her.

"I will understand if you don't. It's a lot to ask." He frowned. "I hate for you to think badly of me, but it's necessary for you to have all the information. He finished brushing her hair. It shimmered in the fading sunlight. "You and I have to rely on each other to get out of this mess. You have to trust me and let that stubborn streak you are so fond of go."

"I'm not making any promises." She sighed and glared at him. "I am not stubborn."

He laughed. "*Cara*, trust me. You are by far the most obstinate woman I have ever met." He leaned down and kissed the tip of her nose. "But don't worry; I rather like that side of you."

She folded her arms across her chest. "Stop that."

"What?" His eyebrow rose. "I've done nothing."

She stomped her foot and glowered at him. "Quit making me like you."

Women. Would he ever understand them? "Maybe you should accept what is between us and make things easier on yourself."

"I wouldn't know what you could possibly mean."

"Perhaps it would be better to show you…"

Damian pulled her into his arms and found her lips with his. A small gasp fell between her lips allowing him to take advantage of her open mouth. He touched her tongue with his. She tentatively touched his in return.

That's it, cara. *Let me in.*

Damian deepened the kiss. He cupped her breasts in his palms. She moaned as he continued his ministrations. If he pushed a little bit he could have her— but he didn't want her like this. They may be living on borrowed time, but he would rather her not regret being with him. Pearla deserved to be wooed.

With every ounce of control he could muster, he pulled back. He groaned at the sight of her. Her lips were plump from his kiss and her cheeks were flushed a bright pink.

"Why did you stop?" Her breaths were ragged as she spoke. It made him want to pull her back into his arms all over again. Every inch of her screamed her desire at him. His self control was close to toppling over the edge.

"You deserve better than a quick tumble on a tiny cot in a dark musty cabin. When I make love to you, *cara*—and I will be on a soft bed with at least a hundred candles lit so I can look my fill."

Damian had to remind himself over and over again why it was not a good idea to give in to their mutual desire. Pearla was so damned pretty and delectable. He closed his eyes and took a deep breath. When he opened them again, he had to clench his hands into tight fists or he'd have pulled her back into his arms again. Being a gentleman was so bloody difficult at times.

Her eyes softened. "Maybe one day I will let you do that too. But you were right to stop this now. I want so much more than to lose my innocence in a hasty act of foolishness."

"Oh, *cara*, trust me, there would have been nothing hasty involved."

She smiled. "If it makes you feel better to think so."

Damian cursed. It was as if she was baiting him to give in and make love to her. He couldn't allow her to gain the upper hand. He meant what he said. Pearla should be loved properly. He still wasn't sure he was that man, but he wanted to be.

"*Cara...*"

The door swung open, and they both turned to see who was barging in on them. Damian frowned.

A dirty man with a full black beard filled the doorway. "Oh, good, you're both awake. The captain has something planned for you both tonight. Come with me. You both are about to witness something you will never forget."

Damian cursed. Whatever it was, it couldn't be good.

CHAPTER THREE

The dirty-bearded bosun who'd leered at her when she boarded the ship gripped Pearla's arm and yanked her forward.

"Let me go," she demanded.

"Sorry, missy, captain's orders. You're coming with me."

Pearla wrenched her arm free and stumbled backward. Her backside hit the floor. She winced as pain shot through her. Damian helped her to her feet.

"It'll be all right, I promise," he whispered in her ear.

Pearla didn't believe anything would ever be all right again. She wasn't about to start giving herself false hope. No doubt Damian sought to give her

some kind of comfort, but she knew better. Whatever the captain had planned was not good. She
wanted to delay it as long as possible. If it meant she
had to scratch the eyes out of the disgusting man in
front of her, she would. It was quite clear what he
wanted from her. If he got his way, he'd happily
debauch her. There wasn't a chance in hell she'd go
anywhere with him willingly.

"Having some problems, Perry?"

Pearla's gaze shot upward at the sound of a new
voice joining the bosun. It appeared their luck was
running out—if they ever had any to start with. The
burly man had friends to help force them on deck.

"I can handle the chit. I like my women a bit
feisty."

"Hurt her and you will die." The tone of Damian's
voice was a combination of rigid and lethal. Pearla
swung around to gaze into his silver eyes. She
believed he was capable of murdering them all, if
only he was at full strength. Unfortunately, he was
still healing from the beating he'd taken a few weeks
ago. Their time locked in the cabin had allowed him
some time to heal, but she didn't believe it was
enough.

"Don't worry, Conte. Your time will come soon
enough." The bosun leered at them both. "You two,

help him topside." He gestured toward two sailors standing nearby. "The missy and I will follow shortly behind you."

Pearla shuffled her feet backward. She couldn't let the evil man anywhere near her. If she did, he'd get his way. The very idea of having him touch her in any way made her skin crawl. Disgust wrapped itself around her stomach as she fought dry heaves. He stalked toward her, preparing once again to grab her. He took two steps, his gaze filled with licentious intent.

The bosun made one fatal mistake. He hadn't allowed the other two men to help Damian topside before he made advances on Pearla. Without any hint of his intent, Damian's fist flew through the air and landed square between the bosun's eyes. Perry's eyes rolled back, and he crumpled to the ground with a loud *thud*.

"Bloody hell." One of the sailors scratched his beard as he studied the bosun's unconscious body. "I suppose we'll have to leave him here for the time being. Someone else can drag his stupid arse out of the room. I'm not doing it"

His co-conspirator nodded at him and then at Damian. They both lunged and grabbed him. One held his arms around his neck in a chokehold. The other held a knife to his gut. "Make one wrong move, and you will bleed like a stuck pig."

Damian held his body completely still. What a mess. How were they going to get out of this now? Pearla bit her lip as she studied the two ruffians. They looked like they'd studied at the school of pirate comportment. There wasn't a doubt in her mind they would kill them both if they believed them to be a threat.

"Now, missy, don't be getting ideas. We don't particularly want to upset the plans the captain be having, but don't make the mistake of thinking we won't kill you and throw your body overboard. If you want your friend here to live to actually see the deck, then you best follow behind us all nice like."

All the warmth she had in her body seemed to drain right out of her. If she were to look in a mirror, she'd probably be as pale as the white clouds floating in the sky. She nodded her head at them. Now was not the time to put up a fight. Besides it was the bosun who'd meant to ruin her. These men wanted them to go meet with the captain. Whatever he had planned couldn't be as bad as what the bosun had meant to do to her.

"I'll do as you ask." Her lips wobbled as she spoke. No. That wouldn't do. They couldn't know how much their actions struck terror in her soul. She squared her shoulders and tried to show no fear. "Please be careful where you stick that blade. You might accidentally poke a hole in Damian, and that would be quite a bloody mess."

Damian's lips twitched as he fought a smile. He rolled his eyes. "Nice of you to show such concern for my well-being."

She snorted. "Who said anything about caring what happens to you?" She raised an eyebrow. "I rather not deal with the repercussions of your imminent demise. I only have one dress, and it wouldn't do to walk around in my chemise the rest of the journey."

The bosun already had issues keeping his hands to himself. She didn't need to give him any more ideas. She didn't want Damian hurt—truly—but she also had to think of what would happen to her if something nefarious happened to him. He appeared to be the only man on board concerned about her welfare. He was also all that stood between her and the evil intentions some of the sailors directed at her. As much as she hated to admit it, she needed him. They were stuck together, and she depended on him.

"You wound me." His eyes sparkled with

mischief. "If we were alone, I'd remind you how much you would care if something happened to me."

The charming rogue had a valid point. She'd desired him more than she wanted to admit. She'd enjoyed his kisses and wanted to see where they would lead. If he hadn't stopped, they'd have gone a lot further in their exploration of each other. A fire had ignited within her that she'd never experienced before. Damian's touch only made her crave more. He was too handsome, and alluring for her poor female heart to withstand. He didn't need to know the full extent of the temptation he presented.

"But we aren't alone, are we?" She tilted her head and held back the smile that threatened to form on her face. What was it about this man that amused her so? "Gentleman I believe you were leading us up to the deck. What does the captain have planned to entertain us? Remind me to lodge some complaints about the accommodations. When I secured passage aboard this ship, I thought I'd have a cabin to myself. It's completely unacceptable that he not only stuffed me in a room with another passenger, but a male one at that. It's going to ruin my impeccable reputation."

Both men's mouths fell open in shock. Good. If she kept them guessing, they wouldn't have time to think about what they might or might not do. She didn't even know exactly where they were. Somewhere in the massive ocean—they could only hope they were somewhere near land.

"Where exactly are we heading anyway?" Both men stared at her blankly. She snapped her fingers and waved in front of their faces. "Can you hear me?"

"I don't understand your question," one of them finally answered her.

She rolled her eyes. "Are you two imbeciles? What port?"

"Oh...um..."

Damian started laughing. One of them punched him in the gut, resulting in some harsh coughs. Pearla wanted to smack some sense into him. Why was he acting like such a bloody idiot? Surely he knew what he provoked with his projected amusement. He must be insane. It was the only explanation for his behavior. If he kept up his current demeanor, they'd murder them and toss them overboard.

"Do you have a death wish?" Pearla stomped her foot. "Do you not at least feel the pointy object in the vicinity of your gut?"

"Oh, I feel it," he wheezed out. "If you don't want me to laugh, then quit making jests."

"I didn't think that was a joke. I truly want to know where we are headed."

Information was power. She wanted to gain all the advantages she could. It was the only way they would have any chance of escaping. She would not spend years imprisoned as Damian's sister Rubina had. There was too much life in her to be stifled in such a way.

"Quit your jabbering and walk in front of us." The man gestured with his head.

"But I don't know where I'm going..." These two were actually idiots. How was she to lead when she didn't know the ship?

"Start walking. We will give you directions as we go."

"Hmmph. Fine." Still didn't make sense to her. What did they think she'd do if she followed? Walk into a different room below deck and disappear? What good would that do? Someone would find her eventually and stuff her back in the room with Damian. If she were being honest with herself, she was glad she had him for company. He made her feel...safe.

Pearla stepped out of the door and eased her way down the dark passage. There had been only one way to turn outside of the door. She had forgotten the cabin was at the end of the passageway. How long had they been locked in that cabin? She'd stopped counting days a while ago. She knew it was weeks…but what if it had been longer.

"Keep going straight."

"Where else am I going to go?" How bloody stupid were they? "It's not as if there are any other passages I could accidentally go down."

"Keep your trap shut and move."

They got irritated rather easy. Maybe she should talk more and put them further on edge. No. If they got too mad they might stick Damian with that knife just because they could. She couldn't risk it. Chatting for the sake of ticking them off wouldn't do them any favors.

"Turn left and follow the ramp up."

Pearla did what he told her to and followed the ramp all the way until they hit the deck. The sun was low on the horizon. If only they could have been topside to see it high in the sky. The little bit of light that came through the porthole wasn't nearly enough. They had very little, and when the sun fell each night the moonlight was a poor comparison.

She stopped in front of the ship's railing. Surely they didn't expect her to walk right overboard.

Pearla peeked over her shoulder. They dragged Damian over and shoved him next to her.

"Don't even think of doing something stupid, Conte. Captain Blythe will be here shortly to deal with you both." The crew members kept close eye on them, not leaving their side.

Where did they think they could possibly go? "Is he going to make us walk the plank?" Pearla asked.

"*Cara,* please don't give them ideas."

She turned and glared at Damian. "I told you not to call me that."

He shrugged. "I doubt I will stop any time. You might as well get used to it."

"Nice to see you both getting along." Captain Blythe strolled over to join them. "It will go well with what I have planned."

Damian's lips formed a firm, straight line. His eyes appeared to shoot daggers at the captain. It was evident he wanted to let loose every ounce of fury inside of him on the wretched man. Pearla wouldn't stand in his way. She wanted to push him overboard herself.

"What, no questions?" Captain Blythe's eyebrow rose. "As chatty as you two were before, I thought at least one of you would ask what tonight's festivities were going to be."

Oh, hell. From the tone of his voice something bad was about to take place. What *did* he have planned? For the life of her, she couldn't figure the captain out. Nothing made sense to her since she'd been locked inside the cabin. She needed answers. This debacle had to end.

Damian's chin jutted out with defiance. He wouldn't be asking anytime soon. So that meant Pearla would have to do it.

She studied her fingernails, acting as blasé as possible. Her head shot up and a smile of feigned joy lit her face. They had no idea what she was capable of. If she had to act helpless and stupid, she would. "Are we having a party?" She clapped her hands with false excitement. "Wonderful. Why didn't you two oafs say so? I'd have skipped happily up here. Do you have musicians? I'd love to dance and have some food and champagne." Pearla shot the words off in a rapid succession, only barely stopping to take a breath. She paused and surveyed the deck. "What, no decorations?"

Captain Blythe's laugh was full of menace. "Conte Leone, I'm going to enjoy tying you to this birdwit for the rest of your lives."

How dare that odious man insult her! She was not the moron in their situation.

He was for not seeing she was playacting. One she had to continue. It wouldn't do to let him see her for who she really was. She squeezed her eyes together with contrived confusion. "Who's a bird-wit? Can you bring my trunks up? And maybe a bath too. If we're having a party, I'd like to get ready. It's been so long since I was able to do something fashionable with my hair."

Captain Blythe shook his head, and his laugh echoed loudly on the wind.

"What do you mean by tie me to her for the rest of my days?" Damian finally asked, his tone harsh. His face was devoid of emotion. The charming rogue was gone and replaced with a man who faced danger on a regular basis. Pearla repressed a shiver. What was he thinking?

"Oh, it's simple enough. You two are getting married—tonight."

Her mouth fell open at the captain's words. Surely he was jesting... Marry Damian? *No. Not. Happening.* She gritted her teeth together. How were they going to get out of this debacle?

CHAPTER FOUR

"*I* must have heard you wrong." Damian paused to let the captain's word sink in. "I swear you said something about getting married."

Damian didn't intend to ever get married. He liked Pearla well enough, but he didn't want or need a wife. Was this the nefarious plan Paolo hatched to ruin Damian? How was an unwanted marriage supposed to destroy him? None of it made sense. Captain Blythe played with his beard and laughed. Damian fought the urge to punch him in the face. Maybe if he broke his nose it would improve his visage. No. Nothing would make the dirty bastard look any better. Acting rashly wouldn't get them out of whatever the captain had planned.

"You heard correctly, Conte Leone." The captain's

grin grew ever wider. "I get the honor of performing the ceremony."

Damian gritted his teeth. "On whose authority?"

"You know who. Don't worry, it will be relatively painless."

Pearla waved her hand. "Excuse me." Her voice was pure ice, as she glared at them all. "Don't I have a say in this?"

"Not at all, missy. Best be prepared to get hitched to the man you've spent weeks locked away with. Your reputation is in tatters. We're doing you a favor."

She snorted. "Please don't. I'd rather not get married today—or any day."

Damian's thought process mirrored hers. A wedding was not something he'd foreseen or even wanted. He still couldn't figure out why Paolo of Captain Blythe thought it would hurt them. Well, besides the fact neither one of them wished to enter into a union of any sort. As much as it pained him to admit it though, the captain had a valid point. Pearla was indeed ruined, and while he'd not intended it, his presence was a direct result of it. He had to help repair the damage. A wedding was the only option they had left to them.

"Too bad. You're going to get married whether

you like it or not." The captain growled. "Now prepare to become blissfully wed."

"I decline." Pearla replied, her tone dripping with disdain. "I think I will return to those wonderful accommodations you have prepared for us."

Pearla turned to head below deck. Damian grabbed her wrist and held her in place. "Don't push your luck, *cara*."

A bad feeling festered in his gut. Damian didn't want to find out what would happen if they didn't go along with the captain—and Paolo's—reprehensible plans. A marriage could be undone, but dead was dead. You didn't come back from that. Pearla must be made to see reason. Their marriage would benefit her. They didn't have to act on it, but for appearances sake it would help her. One day they could find a way to dissolve it and move on with their lives. For now though, it had to happen if they would have any future at all.

"Let me go." She yanked at her wrist. "I'm not marrying you, and they can't make me."

Damian stared down at her and considered his options. They didn't have many.

"But I can," the captain interjected.

"How?" Pearla asked mulishly.

"It's simple. Either you marry him or you die?"

Pearla folded her arms across her chest and glared at the captain. "Kill me then. I will not bend to any man's will."

Damian groaned. "Don't give the man permission to end your life. Would it be so bad to marry me?"

He knew he wasn't a duke, but surely being tied to him couldn't be all bad. He could provide for her and give her a life she was accustomed to. There were plenty of woman who'd found him attractive. Pearla wasn't immune to his charms. She'd fallen willingly into his arms not too long ago. Her moans told him a different story than her current objections. Why was she putting up such a bloody fight over a wedding?

"Yes." She didn't even turn to look at him. Her gaze was unwavering as she shot daggers at the captain. "I made up my mind; I will never marry. One humiliation in my lifetime was quite enough."

"If you don't value your life, perhaps you value his." The captain nodded to one of his men standing next to Damian.

"What do you..." Pearla gasped as one of the men held her arms at her side. "This is outrageous. What could us marrying have to do with you or your despicable boss?"

"It matters not. He wished to see it done, and it's

my job to see it through." The captain replied, his voice harsh. "Don't worry your pretty little head about it. In time, you will understand everything."

One guy held Damian and the other held a knife at his throat. "Say the word, Captain, and I'll slit his throat."

Pearla gulped, her face whitening as she stared at Damian.

"Don't worry about me, *cara*. Do what you feel is best."

"You expect me to watch them kill you?" Her lips trembled. "What kind of person do you think I am?"

Damian didn't want her to feel responsible for him. He'd prefer not to die, but he didn't want to see her hurt any further. What Noah had done...Was unavoidable. He didn't know his wife still lived. That didn't erase the pain Pearla felt because of it.

"If you don't want to get married, we won't," Damian said firmly. Even if he believed it would be for the best. He'd never forced a woman to do anything she was unwilling to do. He wasn't about to start because a mad man held a knife at his throat.

The captain walked over to stand in front of them. "The little lady still seems to be reluctant. Perhaps something worse than death would persuade her to go along with the ceremony."

Pearla's gaze flew to the captain. "What do you mean?"

"I can arrange for my men to each have a turn with you. They've been itching to see what it's like to have a go between your lily white thighs. One word from me, and it will happen. I'll even force Conte Leone to watch."

Damian didn't think Pearla could get any whiter —he'd been wrong. With his fists clenched tight against his sides, he took a deep calming breath. The captain needed someone to break his face in more than one spot. Death would improve his disposition.

"I will decline your generous offer to watch your men debauch Miss Montgomery." Heat fused through his face. "Go ahead with your wedding. I think you've made our positions quite clear."

"You're both willing?" Captain Blythe asked. "I want to make sure we all understand what is at stake."

"We understand," Pearla muttered.

"Get on with it, man. I would like to return to the pleasant cabin you have been keeping us in." Damian's voice reverberated with barely contained fury.

This day was not one he'd soon forget. After all, it wasn't every day a wedding was forced upon him. He wanted it over with. When he was free, he'd enact his revenge. Now wasn't the time to see it through.

The captain laughed. "In a hurry to enjoy your wedding night? Say no more." He winked. "I know how much you've been looking forward to this. I will keep things simple."

What nonsense was the captain spouting now? Looking forward to his wedding night? He almost acted as if they'd planned this farce of a wedding together.

"Are you ready to become a wife?" He turned to Pearla.

She remained mute. A puzzled expression filled her face. "What has Damian been looking forward to?"

"Don't listen to him, *cara*." Damian shook his head. "He's clearly inebriated or has lost his mind."

Whatever game they were playing had taken a different turn. Damian was as confused as Pearla was. He just wanted to be done with them all.

"Oh, you know what I'm referring to conte." He shielded his mouth with his hand, and in a loud whisper said, "Don't worry. Your secret is safe with me."

Damian scrubbed his hand over his face. "Can we

move on? I'm not even going to pretend I under-stand what you're doing."

"Never let it be said I won't help a friend in need." The captain laughed, and gazed at Pearla. "Do you take Conte Leone as your husband?"

Right. Friend. He rolled his eyes, and waited for Pearla to answer the captain. Damian took a deep breath. If she didn't agree to the wedding, he didn't know what he would do. He couldn't watch the crew violate her. She had to say yes. It was the only answer that was acceptable. He understood her reservations. Honestly, he did, but in light of their choices, she had to let them go. They had no choice.

"It's a simple yes or no Miss Montgomery, or would you like to revisit the other options?" the captain asked.

"No."

"No, you won't marry him?"

She shook her head. "I don't need to go over what will happen if I don't marry him."

Damian let out a breath he hadn't realized he'd been holding. For a minute there he thought he'd become witness to a tragedy. Thank God she'd come to her senses.

"Then let's begin again. Release the conte so he can stand beside his bride."

The captain motioned to the man holding the knife to Damian's throat. He stepped next to Pearla and brushed her cheek with the back of his hand. Her skin was cold against his warmth.

"It'll be all right. I promise," he whispered.

Pearla shook her head, shifting her gaze away from his. It broke his heart in two. They could have had something. He saw it clearly now. If they'd been allowed to explore what was happening with them without interference, their life would have taken a different direction. Now he didn't think she'd ever be able to trust in him—in the blossoming desire building between them.

"Isn't he sweet, Miss Montgomery?" The captain laughed. "See, he will be a devoted husband. You won't have to worry for *anything*."

"Please, keep your opinions to yourself. I've agreed to this farce of a wedding. Let's not add anymore." Damian glared at the captain. "I've had enough of your drivel for a lifetime."

"Since you're in a hurry, we will continue." The captain turned toward Pearla and asked. "Will you take Conte Leone as your husband?"

"I will." Her voice was barely above a whisper.

Time stood still as Damian stared down at his soon-to-be wife. Her gaze met his. It was filled with resignation and a tinge of defeat. Her mouth fell with a hint of sadness. He vowed to find a way to erase all her pain. The breeze blew her blonde hair around her shoulders. He reached over and brushed one of the curls with his hand. There were worse fates than to be tied to a beautiful woman. They'd figure out what it all meant later.

"Good. Now, Conte. Do you take Pearla as your wife?"

Damian closed his eyes and realized he actually did want to marry her. It shouldn't have gone this way, but this was a gift in a time of total bleakness. Sadly, it would take time to get his bride around to his way of thinking.

"I will." His voice was clear, concise, and full of conviction.

"Then, by the power granted to me as captain of this vessel, before God and these witnesses, I now declare you man and wife. I'd say you may kiss the bride, but I don't think that's a good idea at the moment. I don't want to get the boys all randy by watching you claim your woman." He nodded to the men holding the two of them in place. "Escort the Conte and Contessa to their room."

A rumble of thunder boomed overhead. Damian's gaze shot upward as a torrential downpour descended from the sky. He cursed. The look of the clouds above him told him they'd better prepare for a hell of a storm. The sooner they got below deck the better. He hoped Captain Blythe and his crew were prepared to battle the sea and sky.

The men pushed them down the ramp leading toward their cabin. When they reached the room Damian went in willingly, Pearla close behind him. The door shut with a *thud*, the key turning in the lock.

There was little light in the room. Damian could barely make out Pearla's silhouette in the darkness. The sounds of her crying devastated him. He made his way to her side and pulled her into his arms.

"Sshhh, *cara*." He soothed her with tenderness. "It's going to be all right. I promise."

Her fists beat against his chest as her quiet weeping turned to howling. "No, it won't. It will never be right ever again. We. Are. Married. How are you not as angry as I am?"

At first he had been. He didn't like being forced to do anything against his will. Now...it seemed right. He knew it would take time and gentle coaxing to convince her it was for the best. Luckily, he was a patient man. He would woo her, and one day maybe they could have a real marriage. For now, they had bigger problems. The largest being how they were going to escape from the ship. They had to be nearing land soon. With the storm raging above them, it couldn't happen soon enough.

"I fail to see why you are so upset." He shrugged. "Marriage isn't a fatal wound."

Her chin tilted up. Probably in defiance. His wife was a stubborn chit.

"No, it is much worse than that. It is a lifetime of torture." She pushed back on his chest to get out of his embrace. "I didn't want this."

Damian sighed. "*Cara,* we were both forced into this marriage. The difference between you and me is I'm willing to let it go and move forward. You keep harping on what can't be undone."

"This night can never be undone, but our marriage can. I will see to it as soon as I escape this hell ship." Pearla seethed. "If you think you are getting a wedding night, you are sadly mistaken."

He shook his head. "I never asked for one."

"Good because you will never touch me again." Her teeth chattered as she shivered.

The ship swayed violently, causing her to tumble forward, landing squarely in his arms. Damian's mouth twitched into a smile. He sent up a silent thanks to the storm for forcing her to be where he needed her. Her safety was his priority, especially now that they were wed. The rain splattering loudly against the ship told him the storm was in full force. They should bunker down for the night to ride it out. If she were to stay by his side, it would make his job much easier, as well as help keep her warm. Her body shook inside his arms. "We're going to die tonight, aren't we?"

"No, we have too much to live for. We should remove some of this wet clothing and get warm under the blankets." He motioned to her. "Come, *cara*, let's take cover on the bunk."

"I told you, I am not letting you make love to me." Her voice was full of scorn. "I will not be your wife in truth."

"You *are* my wife in truth." He frowned. "But to ease your fears, I will not make any demands of you. I don't want you in my bed out of obligation." He rather liked it when the women he bedded enjoyed it as much as he did. He looked forward to experiencing desire with her. She may have been willing to marry Noah and provide him an heir for a sense of duty, but Damian wanted more from a wife. Especially one he never expected to have.

Damian hoped to ease her fears. He spoke the truth. When—and there would be a when—he made love to Pearla, she would be a willing participant. He did not force himself on reluctant women. He didn't need to. There were more than enough women who desired to join him in his bed. It should irk him that the only woman he now desired didn't want him, but he never backed down from a challenge. Everything his pretty little wife did was exactly that. They would live a very interesting life together, provided they got the chance to live it.

"I mean it." She reminded him. "I will not lay with you."

Damian smirked. She might believe what she was spouting off, but he knew it wouldn't take much to change her mind. His wife had conveniently forgotten how she'd gotten lost in his kiss previously.

"This whole situation is far from proper." She nodded. "But you're right. We'll catch our death if we stay in wet clothing."

"True" His mood lightened. "But not everything is out of our control. Whether or not we enjoy each other is totally up to us. If you don't want to know what it is like to feel true pleasure, then that is your choice."

Pearla turned her back to him. "As long as we understand each other. Please unlace my dress."

He moved behind her, and kissed her shoulder. "When you're ready all you have to do is say the word. For now, we will only seek the warmth our bodies need to survive."

Damian slowly undid her laces, leaving them gaping open. She slid the dress off letting it pool into a pile on the floor, her delectable body only covered by a thin chemise. He stood rooted in one spot, clenching his fists against his side as he fought his desire. He'd promised he wouldn't act on his impulses, and he intended to keep his word. Pearla picked up her dress and draped it over a chair. She turned toward him. Her gaze met his and she gasped. The sun had fallen and they had almost no light, but the desire in her eyes was a flame that called to him. He must resist.

"Are you going to remove your wet clothing?"

Damian groaned. He was doomed to fail. "Yes," he croaked. He quickly removed his wet clothes, leaving his underclothes on, and set him near hers to dry. Each movement designed to keep his hands from seeking her delectable body.

"I'm getting chilly. I think you're correct. We need to seek warmth before we freeze." Pearla rubbed her shoulders.

Damian closed his eyes and took a deep breath. He could do this.

"Come. Let's get comfortable. The storm might last for hours, even days."

He led her to the bed and sat down. She remained quiet, but sat down beside him. Damian's lips tilted into a half-smile. He'd given her something to think about. The kiss they'd shared had been more than pleasant. Perhaps he should remind her—no he would respect her wishes. If she wanted to kiss him, he wouldn't stop her though.

"I will know pleasure one day." She blurted. "It just won't be with you."

The hell it won't. "If you say so *cara.*"

"I do. You will never know any kind of pleasure with me." Her voice was firm.

The shipped rocked violently causing them to fall backward on the bed. Pearla crawled on top of him and hid her head against his shoulder. He wrapped his arms around her hugging her tight.

"What were you saying?"

"This isn't delight at being in your arms, you oaf." She muttered against his chest. "This is me fearing for my life."

He laughed. "Where I am sitting, this is the

greatest pleasure a man could ever have. I get to hold my wife and comfort her."

"Don't get used to it."

"I make no promises, *cara*."

If he got his way, they'd be spending many nights in the exact position they were in—only with far less clothing. Not that they were wearing much now. There was still enough preventing him from having her naked in his arms. Damian groaned. His wife had no clue where his mind was wandering. It was for the best. If she knew, she'd move away from him, and that would defeat his purposes. One day she would willingly fall into his arms. It was one promise to himself he intended to keep.

"Oh, be quiet, Damian. I like you much better when you don't open your mouth."

He chuckled lightly. "Settle in and get comfortable. I have a feeling this storm is going to last all night."

Damian wanted to tell her he could do a lot of things with his mouth she'd enjoy quite a bit, but he knew when to hedge his bets. This was not an argument he would win at that moment. For now, he'd gladly settle for holding her in his arms throughout the night.

armth flowed over Pearla, and she snuggled closer into the epicenter of it. She'd never been able to get this warm in her bed before. It was so cozy and solid—wait... Her eyes flew open and met Damian's silver ones. Light danced against them making them sparkle.

She jerked out of his arms and wiped the drool off of her chin. How embarrassing. Damian didn't appear to be ruffled in the slightest. Her eyes narrowed as she studied him in the low light and frowned. How could he look even better than before? For that alone, she could learn to hate him. No one should look that good considering all they'd been through. Damian was too damned sexy.

"Good morning, *cara*...or rather, I think it is morning. The sky is still rather dark and brooding."

The storm had raged forever. Pearla didn't know how many days it went on. The ship rocked and rolled through the furious waves and torrential rain. For a while, though she'd never openly admit it, it seemed as if they were headed toward certain death.

"How long have I been asleep?" Sleep had been nearly impossible, so she was surprised she slept at all. "My body is one big ache." Pearla stretched her arms high above her head and relief filled her sore muscles.

The whole time the ship rocked, she'd been fighting the urge to lose the contents of her stomach. How Damian managed to not get even slightly queasy she'd never understand. On the way home, and she *would* return to London at some point, she'd book passage on a steamship. These stupid clipper ships were not pleasant to sail on. She'd only booked passage on one because she wanted out of England as quick as possible.

"A few hours at most." Damian stared at her. "You didn't miss anything important. You needed the rest."

His gaze never left her. A tingly sensation filled her

belly and a different kind of ache throbbed between her legs. Why him? What did he want from her? She didn't care if they were technically married. They couldn't have a real marriage. Maybe she'd been hasty in saying she'd never allow him to touch her. Why not? She didn't plan on marrying anyone else, and she was his wife. It was something to think about anyway.

She shook her head to clear away her train of thought. Damian would want more than she was willing to give. If she went that route. Ground rules and expectations would have to be laid out and fully understood. She wouldn't have him claiming her and thinking he could dictate to her. After the debacle of her failed wedding, she didn't want to take chances on marriage ever again.

"Did you sleep at all?"

Their clothing had mostly dried hours ago. Pearla didn't feel comfortable in just her camisole and pantaloons. She'd dressed as soon as she believed her dress wasn't damp. Damian had followed her lead and donned his own clothes. She'd breathed a sigh of relief when he had. His naked chest was too tempting.

He turned his head and stared out the porthole. "No."

She frowned. "You should rest. We both need our strength to get through this."

"Are you worried about me, *cara*?"

Damn him and his insistence on calling her his darling. Why wouldn't he stop? This was beginning to become a bit ridiculous. How many times would she have to ask him to cease before he honored her wishes?

"Of course not." She huffed and turned her nose up. "Why would I concern myself with your welfare?" She rolled her eyes. Hardheaded males didn't deserve to be worried about, but she was lying. It did concern her that he hadn't rested. They had an escape to plan.

"You want to know what I think?"

"No." *Yes.*

"You want to come back here and lay your head on my shoulder." He leaned toward her. "Give in, *cara*. You don't need to be afraid of finding comfort in my arms. It's my pleasure to ease all of your worries."

"I'd rather not." The idea did tempt her, but she was made of stronger stuff. She could resist Damian. She hoped. She pictured Noah for a moment. Not too long ago she'd been willing to marry him and all it entailed. Now she was Damian's wife. They were so different. The circumstances and the men, Noah had been the man of her dreams. Only it had turned into a nightmare of her own making. She had to be careful she didn't make the same mistake twice. Damian could shatter what was left of her bruised heart. He filled it in ways Noah never had.

He grinned. The tilt of his lips was a lure filled with decadent wickedness. Pearla sucked in a breath and held it. Damn him for being so handsome and sinful. She was a weak woman to want to throw herself in his arms and beg for mercy. Breathe—she reminded herself, and a whoosh of air left her lungs.

"I don't believe you."

Drat it. "Doesn't matter if you do."

He grabbed her wrist and pulled her back into his arms. "I can prove you wrong."

Damian caressed her cheek with the back of his hand. It sent tiny sensations down her face and spread throughout her whole body. Maybe he was right. She should find out what this making love stuff was all about. He did make her feel things she never felt in her entire life. That had to be a good thing right?

"Please don't." *Oh, yes, please do.*

Why was she a jumbled mess of contradictions? *Make up your mind, you silly girl.* These wanton feelings were filling her belly for a reason. Damian's eyes held such promises. She wanted to know what they were, but the proper Pearla put her foot down and prevented it from happening.

He sighed. "I would never force you to do something you didn't want to do."

"Will you make love to me?" The words were out of her mouth before she knew what she was saying. *Damn it.* Had she asked him to... No. That wasn't her voice filling the room. Pearla was imagining things.

His gaze found hers. Damian remained quiet for a long time. At least it seemed like forever. Hell, had she read him wrong? What man would take this long when offered the opportunity love a woman proper?

"I'm sorry, I shouldn't have asked," Pearla stammered through the words and scooted to the edge of the cot. She turned away from him. This was so... humiliating. The idea of finding pity reflecting from his gaze was too much to bear.

"*Cara...*" He reached for her, but she pulled away.

The more distance the better. Pearla knew when she wasn't wanted. She wouldn't beg a man to love her. Self respect was a good thing, and she would keep hers, damn it.

"Forget I asked and leave me alone. It was a

moment of insanity." Truly it had been. What was she thinking?

"Hell, if it was." He spun her around their gazes locking together. His voice was hoarse and thick with an emotion she couldn't identify. "I wanted to make sure you knew what you were asking from me."

"I knew. I changed my mind. Too late. I don't want you anymore." Lies. She might always want this man, but she needed to be stronger than her base urges.

He studied her again. It was disconcerting. What was he hoping to find in the depths of her eyes? Would he know her deepest desires by staring into them long enough? He appeared to find something he liked because a smile grew on his face.

"All right, *cara*. Let me know when you change it back." He kissed her lips lightly and let her go. "I can wait."

Arrogant bastard.

Sunlight streamed through the widow almost blinding her. When had the sun decided to come out and play? The waves were no longer crashing against the ship's hull. She'd been so wrapped up in Damian she hadn't noticed.

"The storm has finally passed," she muttered.

"Three days were too damn long to be at sea in that mess. Thankfully, it is over."

Had it been three days? It seemed like much longer. The crew had given them limited provisions when it first hit and left them alone for the duration. They had other concerns—like keeping the ship afloat. That they thought of them at all was a blessing.

"How long do you think until we reach port?"

Damian shrugged. "I don't know. It's hard to say where Paolo wants us taken."

Pearla crawled next to him and leaned her head on his shoulder. Whatever comfort he offered, she needed it. Their future looked so bleak. As far as she could see from their porthole, the ocean surrounded them. Escaping seemed impossible. How were they supposed to build a life together when they didn't have their freedom? Damian wrapped his arm around her and pulled her close to him, his head tilted against her head.

The door to their cabin flung wide open and slammed alongside the wall with a deafening *thud*. "Don't you two look rather cozy." The bosun came into the cabin followed by his partners in crime. "The conte is needed on deck."

Damian lifted his head but didn't move off of the

cot. "I will have to decline. Tell Captain Blythe to go to hell."

"Is that any way to treat your benefactor?"

He snorted. "Benefactor? Have you been dipping into the rum casks? I think your brain is pickled if you believe that."

The bosun picked his teeth with his fingernails and spit on the floor. Pearla cringed. How charming. Why wouldn't they leave her and Damian alone?

"Damian would rather stay here with me. Run along now. We don't have time for your nonsense." Pearl shooed him with her hand.

"You don't give the orders, missy. Perhaps you need a lesson in respect."

Pearla raised an eyebrow. Did this ruffian think to school her on something as ingrained as respect? He didn't respect anyone, and he wouldn't be teaching her a lesson regarding it. "No, thank you."

He spread his legs apart, evenly balanced and crossed his arms over his chest. "Conte, we can do this the easy way or the hard way. Please choose the hard way. I owe you for knocking me out the other day."

Damian sighed. "What does the captain want now?"

The bosun laughed. "You've had your fun with

your wife. Just as you wanted. It's time to go. We've reached port."

His eyebrows scrunched up. He appeared confused by the bosun's words. Pearla didn't know what to make of it. What fun? They had been dealing with the storm's raging winds and waves on the boat the same as the crew. They didn't get any enjoyment out of it. Did he mean... Pearla started laughing uncontrollable. The wretches believed her and Damian had been rolling around and getting to know each other intimately this whole time. How laughable. The bosun implied Damian had asked for it too.

"I fail to understand your logic." Damian frowned. "Oh, stop laughing, Pearla. It isn't that funny."

"But he thinks..." Laughter spilled even harder out of her. "I'm so sorry." She wiped tears out of the corner of her eyes. "It's ridiculous really."

The euphoria of her laugher was shattered with the bosun's words. "Grab the conte. Captain didn't think he'd leave the lady willingly."

The two ruffians pushed her aside and grabbed Damian yanking him toward the exit. He fought against their efforts every step of the way. One of them lifted his arms and let his fist fly into Damian's face. It stunned Damian, temporarily giving them the momentum to get him out of the door.

"Enjoy your accommodations, Miss Montgomery. You haven't reached your destination yet, but Conte has met his final one."

They meant to kill Damian. She couldn't allow it to happen.

"Where are you taking him?" Pearla jumped off the cot and stormed over to the bosun.

"Don't worry your pretty head about it. Conte Leone is getting exactly what he wanted." He leered down at her breasts. "Maybe you will consider my offer now that you know what a man feels like sliding between your thighs."

Pearla slapped him. An angry red handprint spread across his cheek. "You will pay for that."

"Not today, Perry. Leave Miss Montgomery be." The Captain stepped inside the cabin. "You know what will happen if the duca finds out you harmed her."

The bosun's face paled. Whoever the duca was—Paolo, Damian had called him—scared these men. She gulped. What did he have planned of her?

"Yes, Captain. I understand."

"Good. Go back up deck and help them with the conte's departure."

Perry rushed out of the room, leaving her alone with Captain Blythe.

"What are you doing with Damian?"

Please, don't let him be hurt. He'd come to mean something to her in a short time. They hadn't gotten to know each other under the best of circumstances. She'd hate it if he met a bad end.

He smirked. "You're not worried about yourself? How touching. Things must have progressed rather well between you and the conte."

"What happened between us is not your concern."

The captain could go to the devil for all she cared. He meant nothing to her. Damian did. She still didn't understand her feelings fully. One day she'd like to explore them.

"Isn't it though? I did marry you after all. I'd like to think I did one good deed." His smile was pure evil.

Good deed? He didn't do anything out of the pureness of his heart.

"What do you want?" Pearla asked.

"Nothing at all, my dear. I thought you might want to know that your little escapade was not fully orchestrated by the duca. The conte...Damian as you are calling him, played his part rather well."

Confusion filled her. What was he talking about? What had Damian done?

"I don't understand." None of it made sense.

An even wider grin spread across his face. The captain leaned against the cabin wall and leered down at her. "Then let me enlighten you. Conte Leone paid my crew to beat him up and hold him in here with you. He thought it was a bit of sport to play the hostage."

Damian wasn't the evil one. He wouldn't hurt anyone. It wasn't in his nature. She paused her line of thinking and gazed at Captain Blythe. How well did she know any of these men? She'd never met any of them before she'd embarked on her excursion. Running away from her problems had led her down this path. It was time she faced things head on and got some clear answers.

"You're lying." He had to be. Damian wouldn't do that to her. Would he? He had made it a point to tell her he wasn't perfect, and had used a woman previously. Was that his way of warning her?

"No? How about if I tell you that your marriage isn't real?" Pure enjoyment sparkled out of his eyes.

Rage boiled up inside of her. She clenched her fists against her side. The more he spoke the more she wanted to hit him. The entire farce of a marriage was fake? To what end? "Then why bother with it?"

The captain spoke nothing but nonsense. It was all...wrong.

"So he could have you willingly in his bed. If you were his wife, then why not give yourself to him. He knew it was the only way you'd let him touch you. You are, or rather *were*, a virginal lady, were you not."

That showed what he knew or thought he did anyway. Damian didn't take her virginity. He had been the perfect gentleman, considering. This was all one huge lie, but she didn't know how much of it was. Maybe Damian had planned it all and then changed his mind. Still they weren't married, so she didn't have to worry about dissolving it. If she could get away from Captain Blythe and his crew, she could continue on her sabbatical. She would still need the time to think and figure it all out.

"Again, not your business." Pearla seethed. "This is all rather convenient when Damian isn't here to back up your story."

"He's done with you. Do I need to remind you of the wedding ceremony?"

What was he spouting now?

"I'm not following what you're saying."

"Don't you recall?" He grinned. "I hinted toward his intentions before I asked if you agreed to be his wife."

Wait... He'd mentioned something about helping a friend. That he'd only done what Damian asked of him. Was what he said true? Did Damian intend to use her? Pearla's heart shattered as she recalled their exchange. She'd been so confused, and Damian had appeared equally so. Was he that good of an actor? Could she really trust what she believed him to be?

The captain shrugged. "I've done my duty and told you everything. Now you are free to roam around the ship once we set sail. When we dock again, you are free to leave. We will help you with your trunks at that time."

He turned to leave.

"Wait" Pearla grabbed his arm, attempting to stop him from leaving.

"Yes?" he asked.

"Where are we going?" Why are they doing this?

"You will find out when we get there."

Awful man, why couldn't she know now? It didn't matter. She'd find out when they arrived and deal with it when she had no other choice.

"And Damian?" she asked.

He shook his head. "Is no longer your concern.

You're a free woman, Miss Montgomery. Don't squander it."

Pearla wasn't sure what to make of it all, but Captain Blythe was right. Damian wasn't her concern. They weren't married. He'd left her. Maybe not of his own free will, but he was gone just the same. She couldn't think about what happened to him because she couldn't do anything to help him. Perhaps the captain was telling some of the truth too.

Maybe Damian hadn't really wanted her after all.

And that was what she couldn't let go of. No one truly loved her. Pearla was easily discarded as if without value—forgettable. Why should Damian be any different? It was time to focus on something she *could* do. Pearla was so tired of being left behind. Why did everyone think it was all right to abandon her, break her heart, and toss her aside? She was done being a victim. From that moment on, she'd do everything necessary to protect herself from pain. Agony engulfed her heart for the last time. No man would ever hold the power to destroy her again.

Pearla needed to know what she wanted out of life. Without a man or love.

CHAPTER SIX

*E*ighteen months later

The hot sun poured over his sweat soaked skin. Damian wiped his forehead with his sleeve. Today was the day. He would escape the island of hell Captain Blythe had sentenced him to. Then he would find Pearla.

"Why have you stopped working?" The overseer sneered at him. "No one said you could take a break."

Damian bit back the curse that wanted to spill from his mouth. He needed to be patient for a little bit longer. This island he'd lived on for over a year had a stark beauty to it. It was too bad he couldn't have found it under better circumstances. Paolo's revenge was ultimate. He'd seen Damian as a threat. Instead of killing him, he'd arranged for him to become and indentured servant in Fiji. An archaic system that hadn't seemed to have died yet on the island. They worked him from sunup until sundown. He had no choice and no way to escape. Although, under the laws of his indenture, he'd be free soon. They *had* to let him go.

He didn't know if they actually would. Damian feared they would kill him before allowing him to return to his former life.

"Yes sir." He nodded and returned to pulling weeds strangling the sugar cane growing on the island. It grated him he'd been subjected to becoming nothing more than a servant. This was not how his life was supposed to go. "It won't happen again."

He swallowed the lump in his throat. This whole situation sickened him.

"See that it doesn't."

Damian didn't look up at the overseer again. Their workday was almost over, and he needed whatever strength he could muster to escape. He should be able to walk away free and clear. Paolo would have arranged something dire to happen to him. Deep in his gut he knew he wouldn't make it alive if he tried to leave openly. It had taken him many months to organize a way off the island.

"Pss."

Damian glanced beside him to the man working the field nearby him. His naturally dark skin a couple shades darker than normal from working under the hot sun. Hian had been brought from India to work as an indentured servant. He missed his home and longed to return to the freedom he'd once enjoyed. "What?"

"Is everything set?"

Damian forced a smile away. Hian had become a friend in a place he desperately needed one. They were going to leave Fiji together. A ship awaited them in the harbor. Once they had the cover of darkness, they would board it. His men were waiting for him. The message he'd smuggled off the island finally reached them. Someone had slipped him news of their arrival an hour ago. Relief flooded him with the information he'd be able to see the last of the cursed island he'd been forced to call home for months.

"It is. Now we just need this cursed sun to lower from the sky and allow us to make our own fate."

Hian nodded. "Good. I will be ready."

They worked tirelessly until dusk. It seemed like the minutes dragged on even more now that he knew he'd soon regain his freedom. Damian had started to believe he'd die on the island and never see Pearla again. He dreaded finding out what happened to her. What evil scheme had Paolo had in store for her? His plans for Damian had been horrible, but they could have been so much worse for her.

His wife.

Did she know he still lived? Had this been Paolo's plan all along? Their forced marriage had made little sense to him. Did he want to ensure both Damian and Pearla suffered in a similar fashion as Noah and Rubina had? If so, he was succeeding. Being away from Pearla, and not knowing her fate, was agonizing. He couldn't wait to locate her and ensure for himself she was all right. Would seeing him be a welcome sight? He had so many questions and none of them had any answers. Soon he would get them.

The bell sounded for the end of the day.

"Grazie al cielo." Damian hoped someone up in heaven was listening to all his prayers. He had to thank someone for finally allowing him to escape. Heaven seemed like a good start. He nodded at Hian. "It's time."

Soon they would be enveloped in darkness and using it to escape the plantation. They pretended to follow the rest of the indentured servants toward their little huts to retire for the evening. Most of them would partake in a meager meal and fall asleep soon after. Their work schedule didn't allow for any free time. It was eat, sleep, work, and then repeat each day.

Damian turned his head left and then right. No one was giving them any mind. He gestured toward Hian. They exited to the far left and hid behind some bushes as the rest of the workers walked past them. They used the foliage for cover as they left the plantation. So far no one seemed to have noticed they were gone.

"Where are you two going?" An irritated man called out to them.

Damian cursed. He'd gotten lax. He slowly turned to see the hateful gaze of the overseer. "We thought we could go to the beach and bathe in the ocean."

"You know you're not allowed without supervision."

Of course not. If they were allowed freedom, they might escape. The plantation owners couldn't have that now could they? Damian would not stay on this island another day. He had a life to get back to. A family that missed him, and more importantly a wife he had to retrieve from whatever hell his enemy had sent her to.

"My indenture is over. I am free to do as I please."

"Are you now? I wasn't informed of this." He let his thumbs rest on the inseam of his pants and smirked. "Go back to your hut."

The bloody fool believed because Damian had followed his orders without question he would continue to do so. He didn't know Damian had a reason to fight back. No, that wasn't true. He always had a reason. Now he had the means to travel to his reason for living. Pearla needed him, and he would be there for her.

Damian glanced over at Hian. The man gave a quick, jerky nod. He was ready to assist Damian if needed. With a slow, easy gait, he ambled toward the overseer, giving the appearance he was meekly doing his bidding. When he was beside him, he wrapped his arm around the overseer's neck and squeezed with all his strength. The overseer struggled as Damian held on tight. Hian picked up a large rock and knocked their tormenter on the head. He slumped forward and Damian let him go. His body hit the ground with a soft thud, his breathing slow and even. Good. At least they hadn't killed him.

"Let's get off this damned island." Damian stood and headed toward the harbor.

"You won't hear me arguing with that." Hian smiled. "I've been on this island far too long.

They kept a steady pace, and once the sun had set and the moon shone over head they made it to the harbor. His ship sat docked nearby. They had to board it and set sail.

"Conte Leone."

Damian turned toward the sound of his name and smiled for the first time in days. "Arturo, it's so good to see you. I thought you were dead."

He'd seen Arturo fall before taking his own beating from Paulo's men. They'd bragged about killing him, and Damian mourned his friend. He was relieved to see his Arturo alive and well.

The man grinned. "They tried, but I have a hard head. Makes it even more difficult to kill me."

He pulled Arturo into a firm hug. Damian stepped back and placed a hand on Arturo's shoulder. "I've never been so glad to see someone in my life. It seems you have found your calling. First you rescue my sister, and now me."

"I'm only sorry it took us so long to find you. We had no idea where Paolo sent you or if he'd murdered you. We never stopped looking."

Damian sighed. "Sometimes it might have been easier if he had. It's been hell on this island. I am more than ready to leave. Hian here is coming with us." He gestured toward his new friend.

"They are waiting for us. Let's get you home, Conte."

"No. I have something more important I need to do."

He missed home, or more aptly the comforts it offered. He could do without those for a while longer. The desire to find Pearla was much stronger, and he wouldn't be able to go home without checking on his sister.

Arturo studied him for a few seconds. "What could be more important than returning to Naples?"

"I have to retrieve my wife."

That stopped Arturo short. He opened his mouth, but no sound came out, and then shook his head. "I wasn't aware you'd married."

Damian laughed. "It's a long story. Neither one of us planned on our impromptu ceremony. Come, let's get aboard the ship and I will tell you my tale, and you can tell me yours. I'm curious how you managed to survive."

They crossed the dock until they reached their destination. Damian told him about Pearla and Captain Blythe's forced wedding. He believed the wedding was only one of the means they'd devised to torture him. His worry over Pearla's welfare had nearly driven him insane.

"Pearla was going to let them kill her before marrying me." Damian shook his head with disbelief still coursing through him. "I still don't fully understand her."

"It's my experience that women are creatures men will never understand." Hian stated. "It's best you don't try. It will only lead to a massive head pain."

Damian chuckled. "You're quite right my friend."

"Conte!" The captain of the ship came beside them on deck. "We are ready to set sail. Give me the word."

"Consider it given," Damian replied. "Could you have someone see Hian to where he'll be staying for our journey? I'm sure he would like to rest." They'd worked hard all day, and Damian was surprised they were both still standing.

"The bosun can show him where to go." The captain nodded at the man by his side.

"Come this way, sir."

Hian nodded and followed the bosun below deck. "I will see you later, my friend."

The captain spun on his heels and ordered the crew to set sail. Damian turned toward his Arturo giving him his full attention. "So, Arturo, how did you survive?"

"I was gravely injured." His voice held a morose tone, as he stared into the dark sky. "In truth, I should not have survived. A woman took pity on me and nursed me to health. I've only been healthy enough to aid in the search for you this past month. I didn't have much strength." He lowered his head. "I'm sorry I failed you."

"You did not fail me Arturo." Damian shook his head. "I'm glad you are alive and well. Maybe later you can tell me a little about the woman who saved you."

Damian did not fault him. Arturo had almost given his life in his service. How could he blame him? Still he needed answers. He couldn't go blindly back into the world. When he found Pearla, he'd need to be able to protect her. When it was just him, he'd been careless. He couldn't continue to carry on in that fashion. His wife would have to come first.

"She's amazing. I think you'll like her." Arturo grinned sheepishly. "I plan on asking for her hand in marriage upon our return."

"Good." Damian smiled. "You deserve happiness." They'd all been through a lot at the hands of the duca. It was time to set it all aside and live their lives unencumbered. "Do you have news of my sister or Paolo?"

"I have not seen the Duchessa, but I do know she is well."

That was good at least. His sister was the only other woman who meant anything to him. His mother died shortly after Rubina was born. He barely knew her. He'd focused all his love and adoration on his baby sister.

"Did she and Noah work through their problems?"

Arturo nodded. "My informant tells me that they are very much in love. I thought it best not to approach her until I had news of what happened to you."

"That's probably best." Damian nodded. He knew Rue would be worried about him. They were close, and he'd never come to see her. She would be relieved to see him, but first he must find his wife. If she wasn't already in danger, she could be now that he was free. "And Paolo?"

"He is dead. Your sister shot him with his own pistol."

Relief flooded him. Thank heaven for taking that evil out. He wished it had been him and not his sister, but at least he knew that was one person he wouldn't have to worry about.

"I'm glad he's dead."

"He was an evil man," Arturo agreed. "But just because he's gone doesn't mean that the evil is gone."

Was it too much to ask to have some peace? What new evil had sprung up to ruin all the plans he had for his life? When would they catch a break? Damian was tired of all the drama life kept throwing at him. All he wanted was to find his wife and start a family.

"What do you know?"

"Someone has taken up where he left off." Arturo sighed. "The only difference is they are not obsessed with your sister—they are fixated on you."

Damian whipped his gaze toward him and asked, "Who is it?"

"Your former paramour, Camellia."

He cursed. Damian should never have gotten involved with her. She was only supposed to be a means to an end. The Duca's sister had become infatuated with him. Damian hadn't seen any reason not to court her for information on her brother. It'd been a disaster, and the one mistake he regretted the most.

"What has she done?"

"Nothing as yet. She's been trying to locate you." Arturo looked out across the ocean. "I believe, if we had not rescued you today, she'd have found you within a fortnight. Her brother had made it impossible to find you. Captain Blythe is currently her guest. It won't be long before he tells her all she wants to know."

Captain Blythe was becoming a thorn in his side. He was almost as irritating as Paolo. Why was he suddenly keeping Camellia company? He rubbed his temples as pain shot through his head. Would any of it ever end?

Damian shook his head and sighed. "It might not be as bad as you think."

"No, it is much much worse." Arturo's gaze filled with anxiety. "She wants you. I think the insanity gene has spread through that family. But she is a wicked woman in ways her brother never was. She has strange proclivities…"

He opened his mouth to start asking for details, but changed his mind. He didn't really want to know what Camellia was planning. It was something that could wait until later. When he saw her again he'd deal with her. Maybe if he apologized for his misdeeds she'd let it go. Of course, that would only work if she wasn't crazy like Paolo. He could hope Arturo was wrong in his assessment of her.

"I can't be worried about her. She can obsess over me all she wants. I am taken and do not want her." Damian frowned. "I have bigger concerns than what Camellia wants or desires."

"Your wife?"

Damian nodded. "Yes. She comes first always."

When he closed his eyes he could picture her. He wanted to reach out and stroke her beautiful golden curls and reassure himself she was all right. Once he found her, he'd pull her into his arms and never let go. At least until her stubborn streak found a way to make things difficult. It was one of the things he adored about her. He missed her.

"Then we will find her. Camellia can wait for now," Arturo agreed. "But, Conte, don't think she will forget about you. She will find you, and when she does I fear it won't be a pleasant experience."

Damian didn't doubt Arturo was right. Camellia had always been an odd person. He didn't know what she was fully capable of doing. When he saw her again, he'd discover what her plan was. For now, he wouldn't worry about it. He must locate his wife. Wherever she was, he would find her, and then they would work through this marriage of theirs. They had so much they still didn't know about each other.

"Pearla first, and then I will deal with Camellia."

"I only pray you are not too late… For your wife or handling your former paramour."

Damian stopped and turned his gaze toward Arturo. His words gave him an idea. "Maybe the fastest way to find Pearla is to seek out Camellia. Didn't you say Captain Blythe was keeping her company?"

Arturo nodded. "He is."

"Good. The Captain and I have some things to settle. He will tell me what he did with my wife." Damian grinned. He couldn't wait to see the good captain again and show him how much he'd enjoyed his stay on Fiji. Perhaps he should experience a similar excursion. "Where is Camellia calling home these days?"

"She has been in London since you disappeared. I suspect she knows you will return there before Naples. You have ties there again with Rubina finally returning to her husband." Arturo shook his head. "I don't like any of this, Conte. I have a bad feeling."

Damian shook it off. He couldn't be worried about Arturo's foreboding feelings. If he wavered every time something bad might happen he'd never find Pearla again. "Nevertheless, we will sail to London. Inform the captain of our new destination.

I am going to retire to my cabin. It's been a bloody long day."

Arturo nodded. "I will do as you instructed, Conte. I only hope this goes how you want it to." He turned on his heels and headed toward the captain, leaving Damian to his own musings. Going to London was the only lead he had to finding Pearla. Camellia would make things inherently more difficult. But it was worth every risk he would take. Nothing would stand in his way. Pearla would be with him again, and they would find out what was between them. Their time together had been too short. Arturo's concerns be damned.

Damian sighed. "I'm coming for you, *cara…*"

CHAPTER SEVEN

earla stared across the horizon. The sun had begun its ascent, and glowed brightly as it rose in the sky. She'd be in London soon. The harbor glistened in the distance. She'd been gone from home for so long. A part of her was happy to finally be returning home, but the other part of her dreaded it. What would she find when she stepped back into society?

Hopefully the ton forgot about her botched wedding.

She didn't want to look into the eyes of all her friends and still see pity raining out of them. Pearla had been through a lot in the past year and a half. All of the difficulties life had thrown at her had made her stronger. It was time to return home and face her biggest fear.

Seeing Noah with his wife.

She wanted him to be happy. Truly. But it would still hurt something deep inside to witness it. Pearla had given up on finding that kind of happiness for herself. For a brief moment, she'd thought she could maybe have it with Damian, but he too abandoned her. If Captain Blythe was to be believed, it had all been a ruse. To what end she still didn't know.

"Are you prepared for your return home?"

Pearla turned to the sound of Mason Tennick, The Earl of Addison's voice. His pale blond hair blew in the breeze. His gaze left hers momentarily as he turned to look in the direction that had caught her attention. He had been courting her on the journey. She wasn't a fool. It didn't take much to surmise that he thought she was wife material. What he didn't know was she never intended to marry. She'd tried it once—no…twice, if her fake wedding to Damian counted.

"As much as I can be." She forced a smile on her face.

He turned toward her. Lord Addison did have lovely green eyes. If only she found him attractive enough to marry… Maybe she didn't like blond men.

Her track record surely spoke for that thus far. Both Damian and Noah had dark hair. She found that Noah had begun to pale in comparison though. Her thoughts wandered far more to Conte Leone. She often wondered what he was doing, where he was, and why he'd left her. It didn't help she'd been attracted to him. It appeared he wasn't worth her attention, but she couldn't stop picturing him.

"Don't worry about what all the gossipmongers will say," he encouraged. "You're lovely and what happened at your wedding was unavoidable. No one knew the Duke of Huntly's wife was still alive. Not even he did. They can't hold it against either of you. It was an unavoidable transgression."

Dratted man had to remind her of the one thing she didn't want to think about... Besides Damian anyway. Both Noah and Damian had a lot to answer for in regards to her bruised heart. She never should have let herself fall in love with Noah. Damian had *bad idea* written all over him. He'd been in full rake mode when he was locked in that cabin with her. She should be glad that nothing more had happened between them. A part of her wished she'd experienced what he'd offered her, the other part was thankful she'd never given into that dark desire. The mixed emotions engulfed her every day when

Damian crossed her mind. Why couldn't she forget him?

"I'm no longer concerned about what anyone in the ton has to say about me. I've had time and distance from the situation. It doesn't matter to me any longer." Lies. It all mattered, but she refused to let the world see it.

He smiled. "I'm glad to hear that."

Pearla squashed the desire to roll her eyes. Lord Addison was so tedious to converse with. "Are you happy to be returning to London?"

"I am." He lifted her hand into his own. "But more importantly, I'm hoping to spend more time with you now that we are both back in England."

Pearla wanted to jerk her hand out of his. Why did he think he had the right to touch her at all? She didn't desire any man's attention. She took a deep calming breath and slowly removed her hand from his grasp. She was overreacting. Lord Addison hadn't meant to make her uncomfortable. It wasn't his fault she detested his touch.

"If I attend any social events, please do seek me out." *Please don't. Just forget I exist.* "It will be a pleasure to see you again."

Why did she have to remain polite? This was all an exercise in futility. She had no plans to go out much in society. Pearla would only attend functions to see her closest of friends. Lord Addison didn't even make the list let alone the short one that contained people she liked.

"May I call upon you?"

Pearla's mouth fell open, but she couldn't come up with a reason to deny him. "It is going to take me some time to get my affairs in order. Perhaps after I've settled in…"

"I understand. I will give you some time. Is a fortnight too soon?" Lord Addison brushed a lock of her hair behind her ear. "I hope we will have a chance to know each other much better."

Pearla gritted her teeth. She wanted to smack his hand for his presumed familiarity. Did he think she would fall into his arms because Noah set her aside for Rubina? Perhaps she shouldn't think badly of his intentions, but she couldn't help it. No one was going to consider her so easily discarded ever again.

"Yes. I see." She bit her lip. "Why don't we wait and see if I'm up to receiving then. I'm not sure how long it will take to prepare my house for visitors."

Another lie. Her townhouse was already prepared for her. She'd sent notice to her housekeeper before she even thought about when she'd return home for good. It had been on her mind for some time. The desire to see England and her friends. So she'd asked Mrs. Hopsen to ready her home for her. Not too long after she booked passage on a passenger ship to return. It was time, after all.

Lord Addison smiled. "I hope it is sooner rather than later. You'll send notice if it is?"

Pearla sighed. "If I remember to..." She'd forget on purpose. There was something about him she didn't like. Perhaps because he was a male and breathed. He seemed nice enough to be around, but Pearla didn't want to garner any man's attention.

"Please, say you won't forget about me."

If she had her way he'd already be a distant memory.

She feigned a bright smile. "Of course not... But you know how busy it is to run a household. I might not have time to stop and consider anyone else. You do understand, don't you?" It was getting rather tiresome to continue forged happiness around Lord Addison.

He lifted her hand and kissed her palm. Pearla resisted the urge to shudder. At least she was wearing gloves. It would have been so much worse if his lips had touched her bare skin. She'd had enough of men and their licentious intentions. Lord Addison meant to court and marry her. He'd made his desires known. When she thought of him, pictured his face, or even spent any time with him her insides were nothing but an icy void. She had not one good emotion regarding him.

"I do." His lips tilted into a cocky grin. "Rest assured I'm willing to wait however long it takes for you to allow me to call upon you. You, my dear, are worth it."

Pearla looked away from him and rolled her eyes. Some much needed distance from Lord Addison would be in her future. He'd been a thorn in her side too long already. She sighed and turned toward him. Maybe she should be a little less polite with him. If only she wasn't so well mannered.

"I appreciate your attention, but you should know I don't plan on entertaining much for a while. Being in the company of others is too taxing."

"Surely you can make an exception for me?" He raised an eyebrow. "I'm not just anyone."

His arrogance knew no bounds. She mentally sighed. He wouldn't be so easily persuaded to leave her alone.

She shook her head. "There is a select few I plan on allowing into my life. Friends and family I've not seen for over a year. For now, that will be all I have time for."

"I see." He stared off into the distance.

"Pardon me, Miss Montgomery." Mary Alice, a young maid Pearla hired as a chaperone on her journey approached them. "The captain said we're entering the harbor. Do you still wish me to accompany you?"

Pearla smiled. "Of course. Did the captain indicate how long until we dock?"

"He said within the hour."

Lord Addison interrupted them, "Don't you have duties you need to see to then?"

"I…" Mary Alice muttered. Fear filled her eyes as she glanced over at Lord Addison.

Pearla glanced back and forth between them. What reason would her maid have to fear the earl? Her face had paled considerably when Lord Addison addressed her. Perhaps she was intimidated by a lord, or any man's presence. She was more concerned why Lord Addison felt the need or even the right to order her staff about.

"Mary Alice, go down to our cabin. I will join you in a few moments. We will rest a bit until we dock together." She smiled, reassuringly. "It won't be long before we're safe in my townhouse."

Mary Alice bobbed her head and scampered off. She'd question her maid later. For now, she'd put

Lord Addison in his place. He would understand why he couldn't step in and order her maid. He wasn't anything to Pearla. No man could dictate to her. She was in full possession of her inheritance, and as far as she was concerned fully on the shelf. Marriage was not something she wanted for herself —ever.

"Lord Addison, do *not* order anyone in my employ or question them again. They know what my wants and desires are. I do not need you, or anyone else, to step up and handle my affairs."

He opened his mouth and closed it again. His lips formed a thin white line, the displeasure in his eyes evident as he gazed down upon her. He hadn't liked being dressed down one bit. *Too bad.* Pearla didn't care what he thought of her. Maybe it would give him a reason to quit pursuing her hand in marriage.

"Pardon me," he began, "I was unaware I was overstepping. It won't happen again."

Pretty words, but she didn't believe them. He was saying what he believed she wanted to hear. What he didn't know was it didn't matter if he apologized or not. Lord Addison meant nothing to her. It irritated her that he thought he had a right to step into her life in any way. After they docked, she would go home and not give him another thought.

In fact, if she never saw him again it would be too soon.

"It's all right." It wasn't, but polite Pearla was coming back out again. "Now that you know, I'm sure it won't happen again." She almost snorted at those words. Lord Addison was an overbearing arse. Of course he'd try to dictate to her again. Pearla was beginning to know his type rather well. She'd been living around his type all her life. Her father, Viscount Redding, was a man like him. At least she didn't have to live under his roof any longer. Thanks to her inheritance from her grandmother, she could live on her own and not worry about answering to anyone.

"Of course not." He smiled. "Would you like me to escort you to your cabin?"

The man was persistent. Was he obtuse or did he just not care? Pearla wanted to extricate herself from his company. Allowing him to escort her anywhere would be defeating her purpose. She shook her head. "I can find my own way. Good day, Lord Addison."

He bowed. "Until I see you again, Miss Montgomery."

Pearla smiled and turned away from him. Only then did she let her smile fall. She watched another ship across the harbor head toward the docks. In the distance, the old clipper coasted through the water. She'd never sail on one of those blasted ships again. The steamer she'd secured passage on was not only faster, but it didn't carry memories she'd like to forget—like the type of ship she'd been held hostage on.

She shook her head as a man with long dark hair filled her mind. Pearla glanced back at the ship. It was a good distance away, but she could almost make out some of the individuals on deck. If Damian was amongst them, she'd never know, but a part of her had to wonder. Would he come back to London? At some point he would. His sister lived there.

She couldn't think about what could or would happen when he turned up again. It wasn't a question of if, but when. On that day, Damian would realize he no longer meant anything to her.

If only she could convince herself of that notion.

CHAPTER EIGHT

*D*amian stepped into his set of rooms at the Albany and sighed. It had been a bloody long day. They docked several days ago, and he had immediately begun figuring out where Camellia and Captain Blythe were. They hadn't been in residence when he'd paid a call. He'd been away from London for so long he had no clue what entertainments were being offered. The season was in full swing, and no doubt if anyone knew he was in town he'd soon have undesired guests pouring in. Perhaps he should pay his sister a visit. She could spread word of his arrival and speed up the process.

A boom rattled the room, shaking throughout. He jumped at the sound. He brought his hand up and rubbed his chest to ease his rapidly beating heart.

"Who the hell is visiting?" He marched toward the door and swung it pen and frowned. "Arturo, do you have any news?"

He brushed past Damian and entered his residence. "I do."

"What have you discovered?" A rush of emotion spread through him. "Have you located Camellia or Captain Blythe?"

"I can tell you that they are not currently in London. My contacts confirmed they left the city a few days ago." Arturo headed over to the liquor cabinet and poured brandy into two glasses, handing one to Damian. He took a swift drink and nodded. "The good news is they are still in England. The bad news is they have headed to Somerset for a few days. Camellia had a need to explore Bath."

Damian snorted. "Did she want to take in the waters? Or was it the theater district that appealed to her—she'd make a good actress for them to acquire."

"I wouldn't presume to understand the inner workings of Camellia Fonte." Arturo swallowed the rest of his drink and set it down. "They are expected to return at the week's end. So you just have to sit back and await their return. Perhaps we can use this time to form a strategy on how to best handle the situation."

What was the best way to deal with a former lover? Camellia had gotten rather possessive, so he'd had to break things off with her. It had been a blow to his investigation of her brother to do so, but she'd been too difficult to handle any longer. She was a beautiful woman with inky black hair and sapphire eyes that made it rather easy to fall into bed with her. Damian never saw her as anything but a source in his quest to rid the world of Paolo Fonte. He had done her a disservice.

Maybe the best way to approach her was to apologize for being the rake that ruined her... Somehow, he didn't think it would go over well. Camellia wanted him—what she expected to do with him once she managed to trap him, he didn't know. The element of surprise was their best bet. Damian didn't want to be the fly to her spider.

"Do you have someone working inside her townhouse?" A staff member in their employ would be a useful tool—making it easier to access her home when she least expected it. He knew Camellia well enough to anticipate her moves once he was inside. It was giving her time to plan that would be his downfall.

"One of our people was hired as a footman and another as a maid. It is the maid who gave me the information on their whereabouts. The footman is traveling with them to Bath. He should be able to give us more information about her sudden trip when they return."

"Good. When they return we will act. I need to know where Pearla is. The sooner we can question Captain Blythe the better. Waiting is going to be hard..."

"You will have the information you need to find her. We have to be patient." Arturo walked to the window, and glanced outside. "The past couple of years have been difficult for us. They have not been without good tidings though. Perhaps you should use this time to visit your sister. I believe she's had some happy events you will be interested in."

He raised an eyebrow, questioningly. "What have you learned about Rubina?"

Arturo turned toward him. A small smile was on his face. "Her and her duke are doing well. Though you should realize she has mourned you. It's rather ironic that at one time, albeit different instances, the world believed you both dead, don't you think?"

"They believed I was dead? I thought everyone believed I was merely missing..." Damian frowned.

Why hadn't he asked more questions? He'd been consumed with his own needs and never stopped to think about how his indenture may have impacted his family. "You're right I should go and see her. I wasn't in a hurry with my priorities being focused on finding Pearla. Rubina will be relieved to see me again—much like I was when you brought her to me. It would be selfish to let her to continue to believe I've stopped breathing."

What a mess. Damn Paolo Fonte for playing God with their lives. He had taken Rubina from them for years and had somehow managed to do the same with him. His father probably believed him dead as well. What it must have done to the older man. First his daughter and then his son...

"It's a wise decision to pay a call on her. You should go to her now. Give her my regards when you see her."

Damian nodded. "We will meet later and discuss how to handle Camellia. Captain Blythe isn't going to be happy to see me. He *will* give me the information I need and then we can see about turning him over to the authorities for his crimes." Kidnapping two people shouldn't go unaccounted for. "In the meantime, we will wait patiently and I'll head over to see Rubina. It's past time I inform my family I am very much alive."

"Of course," Arturo agreed. "I will walk out with you."

They left his rooms and strolled toward the building's exit. Once they were outside, they parted ways. Damian decided to walk to Rubina's. He needed the exercise to clear his mind. Finding Pearla had been his sole focus since he'd been rescued. Never once had he thought about his family. His absence probably would have been missed from the start. Rubina had been in danger and expected him to help her. Why had he not considered they might believe him gone for good? Damian had always put Rubina first in the past. Meeting Pearla had switched his focus entirely. He would have to apologize profusely to Rubina when he saw her. He'd been a horrible brother to her.

At least he could be reassured that she was all right and Paolo would never hurt her again. He wished his sister hadn't been the one to send the evil bastard to hell. Damian wanted that privilege. If he could resurrect him and kill him all over again he would. The harm the duca had caused his family... He shook his head to clear his thoughts away. All that mattered was they'd survived and would continue to do so. Paolo hadn't won. His family was stronger than the malice that pursued them.

Damian rounded the corner and headed toward the Huntly townhouse. He stopped short of it and stared at the entrance. There was a bustle of activity surrounding his sister's home. Carriages being moved away as not to block the street and the door opening and closing allowing people to enter...

Was she throwing a party? Maybe it wasn't a good time to visit.

He almost turned around and left. Until he caught sight of the blonde vision he'd been searching for since his escape. Pearla...

She was going into Rubina's house! How long had she been in London? When had Captain Blythe let her go? He breathed a sigh of relief to know she was free. At least that was one less thing he would have to worry about. Now he had to go inside and claim his wife. Explaining his absence to his family could wait. They would understand.

He stalked forward intending to gather Pearla into his arms. He'd missed her and couldn't wait to breathe in her scent again. What she must have gone through after they were separated—he didn't want to think heavily about it. The important thing was she was safe and they could pick up where they left off.

When he reached the entrance, the door flew open. "Good evening," the butler greeted him. "The wedding has already started. His Grace asked that late arrivals wait outside the room as to not disturb the ceremony. After it concludes you may go inside."

Wedding? Who was getting married? It didn't matter. He could be patient for a little while longer. He didn't want to disturb another couple's nuptials. Pearla wasn't going to sneak away on him in the middle of the ceremony.

"That's fine. I can wait."

Damian rushed past him and headed toward the sound of voices. He stopped outside the doorway and watched his sister walk toward Noah. Rubina raised her hand toward her husband. He lifted her hand to his lips, kissing the back of it. They stared at each other for a few moments before they turned their attention to the vicar. It looked as if they were going to renew their wedding vows. Good for them. He was glad they'd found a way back to each other. His sister deserved to be happy.

He tore his gaze away from their exchange of vows and searched for the woman he needed to see the most. Damian found her sitting serenely, watching the ceremony. He had to wonder if it bothered her to see Noah marrying Rubina again. At one time she thought she would marry Noah herself. It must bring back memories observing them now. They glowed with happiness and only had eyes for each other. Pearla didn't look away from them once.

His attention returned back the wedding.

"You may now kiss your bride," the vicar announced.

Noah's gaze never left Rubina. "You don't have to tell me twice." The duke kissed his wife as if he'd never get the chance again.

Now would be a good time to interrupt. Damian's patience had come to an end. He needed to talk to Pearla, and he couldn't wait for Noah to stop kissing Rubina.

"Pardon me for interrupting—I always did show up late for important events."

Noah and Rubina glanced across the room. A gasp of surprise fell from Rubina's lips. Damian strutted into the room with large purposeful strides.

Rubina ran to him and hugged him tight. "I'm so glad to see you. Where the bloody hell have you been all this time?"

Damian hugged her tight in his embrace. He

kissed the top of her head. "Easy now, Rue." He eased back. "I rather like breathing."

"Are you going to answer my question?" She raised an eyebrow.

"I will explain it all at another time." He scanned the guests, locking his gaze on Pearla. "I came for another reason."

Rubina pursed her lips in displeasure. She opened her mouth to speak and then paused to study him. Then she turned in the direction that held him riveted. Damian could tell she was curious and wanted to ask questions. He would tell her about everything later—much later. He needed to wrap Pearla in his embrace and reassure himself she was indeed all right.

Pearla stood up. She glared at Damian. Her hand flew to her chest; her mouth hung open with shock. She shook her head several times as if not believing what she saw in front of her. Damian could relate to what she appeared to be going through. Finally, he'd found her, and they could be together again.

Rubina turned and asked, "Do you two know each other?"

"I think a man would know his wife when he sees her." Damian's gaze never left Pearla.

Pearla's blue eyes were filled with fire as she

stared back at him. She was angry... He couldn't blame her. She probably blamed him for deserting her. When he got her alone, he would explain what Captain Blythe had done. He would never have left her willingly. She'd come to mean the world to him in a very short time.

"I am not your wife," Pearla said with disdain.

Pearla pushed her way past everyone. Bloody hell, he'd have to chase after her. It wasn't going to be as easy as he'd thought. Why would it have been? Pearla was a headstrong woman and wouldn't cave without giving him hell first. If she wanted a fight, she'd get one. Damian was never letting her go again.

CHAPTER NINE

$\mathcal{P}$earla pushed open the front door and flew down the steps. She rushed past one of the footmen and headed toward her carriage. Her heart beat rapidly against her chest, threatening to push right out of body. Her breathing became tapered as she struggled to control her wayward emotions. How could this happen to her? The sooner she put some distance between her and the Duke of Huntly's townhouse, the better. Only then would she be able to breathe and control her racing heart.

She waved toward her driver and stepped inside the carriage. "Take me home now," she demanded.

Damian had shown up. She knew at some point he would. It never occurred to her it would happen almost immediately upon her return to London. Although she *should* have known... She had the worst luck of anyone alive. It didn't matter. She leaned her head against the back of her carriage and breathed a sigh of relief as the carriage began to move. Seeing Damian had put her on edge, but she'd made it out without too much trouble. Soon there would be enough distance between them to alleviate the worst of her wayward nerves.

The door to her carriage jolted open, startling her already rampant heart. Her hand flew to her chest to steady the rush flowing through her.

"You didn't think you'd get away so easily did you love?" Damian closed the carriage door and sat across from her. "We have some things to discuss."

Her mouth fell open as her entire body seized in shock. When would she learn? Nothing was ever a given—Damian was set to prove her wrong at every turn. Why did the world seem to hate her? All she'd wanted was some distance to think before having to deal with this man before her. Was that really too much to ask? Apparently so, because now she was being forced to spend time with one of the men she'd hoped to avoid. She should have stayed abroad. Things were much simpler, and peaceful, when she was on her own.

She pursed her lips in displeasure as she studied him. "Why are you here?"

"I believe I already said why." His smile was cocky, and he seemed so sure of himself.

As far as she was concerned they had nothing to discuss. He said it all when he left her alone on that ship. Whatever the reasons were for him leaving— she didn't care. All she wanted now was to be left alone. They were nothing to each other.

"I beg to differ. I'd be perfectly fine to never speak to you ever again." Ever. He could just hop out of the moving carriage and leave her be. "I'd be much happier if you left me alone."

"We're married—"

She held up her hand. "Let's stop right there. I believe I already told you I am not your wife. So if you're feeling some obligation toward me under that false assumption let me disabuse you of that notion immediately. I don't need you. You are not my husband, and you never will be."

He stared at her. The muscles in his cheeks flexed. His eyes turned to a molten silver as he studied her. She didn't know what it meant or why he wasn't saying anything. She closed her eyes and sighed, gaining the strength to continue dealing with him. Being in Damian's presence affected her on an intimate level. She was drawn to him in ways she'd never been to Noah. Her whole body craved to move closer to him and bask in his warmth. She couldn't, wouldn't, give into that desire—sadly she knew what a disaster it would be to fall into his arms again.

"Explain why you believe we are not married."

Pearla looked up into his eyes. He seemed—resigned. No that wasn't it either… Determined was more like it. Damian seemed to have a single-minded pursuit in mind, and lucky her, she appeared to be the object of his sole focus. She needed to get his train of thought on something other than her.

"Captain Blythe said it was all a ruse." She shrugged. "You can rest easy. We're not, and never have been, legally wed. You're free, Damian. Go find someone else to bother."

She meant what she said. Didn't she? Maybe if he put up more of a fight she'd believe he really wanted her. It was so hard to decipher what was true and what wasn't. Her heart had leapt with joy when she'd laid eyes upon him. Followed by fear—why was he in London now? She'd just decided to return. There must be some other reason.

"You never thought to check to see if he was telling the truth? The man does like playing havoc with other people's lives." He raised an eyebrow.

"You do recall our time together locked in a cabin on his ship, correct?"

How could she forget? It had been one of the worst and best times of her life. She had begun to feel wanted, even important to someone else. Until Captain Blythe added to her already growing self-doubt... Damian didn't want her. He never did. "I remember it in vivid detail."

"So tell me, word for word, what the good captain told you."

She shook her head. "It doesn't matter. None of it does. I am home and free to do anything I want. If you're so concerned about what the captain has done, or did, go find out from him. I'm satisfied knowing I'm not tied to you for the rest of my life."

A sharp sting of pain stabbed through her unsteady heart. That wasn't entirely true. She'd wanted him. Hope had coursed through her body at the idea of him as her husband. Then it all crashed down around her. Why did everyone want to discard her? Damian wouldn't have the power to hurt her ever again. She couldn't let him in only to lose him. It hurt too much the first time. If she opened herself up only to lose him—it would destroy her. She couldn't afford to let herself love him. They'd been doomed from the start.

"It bloody hell does matter." His voice was harsh. "You matter. Don't sell yourself short. We need to know the facts. If we're not legally wed, that can be rectified."

What nonsense was he spouting now? "We're not wed. I have already stated that several times. Nothing needs to be fixed. All I need from you is space. What are you not understanding?"

"We belong together, *cara*." His grin was wicked as his gaze raked over her. "We were inevitable from the start. It's only a matter of time until you're fully mine."

She snorted. He was ridiculous. They were not inevitable. Nothing ever was. This discussion had gone off course and derailed into a subject she didn't want to take part of any longer. Damian needed to find someone else to harass.

"I will never be yours. That ship sailed." In more ways than one. She leaned forward and stated firmly, "I'm not, nor will I ever, belong to you. Get acclimated to that now. You do not have any thing I need or want."

His lips formed a grim white line as anger flashed through his silver eyes. "I refuse to accept that."

"That's your problem, not mine. I've accepted we were not meant to be together months ago. I'm only surprised you haven't reached the same conclusion." This had reached beyond tedious. She waved her hand with frustration. "I deserve better. You're not the man for me."

He stayed silent again. How could he hold his anger in? His body remained completely still as he studied her. He must want to lash out. She had not been nice, and held nothing back from him. She had not lied. She did deserve better. Damian had already proved she couldn't depend on him. He only wanted her because he believed she belonged to him. Pearla belonged to no one, and especially not to a man who would readily abandon her for his own selfish pursuits.

"I understand," his voice was eerily quiet and firm. "You wish to be courted."

No. She wanted to scream at him, but she held it back. Her voice shook with raw emotion as she explained, "You understand nothing at all."

"Oh, I think I do." His smile grew on his face as he continued to stare at her. "You think no one could ever truly want you. Your answer is to push me away so your already bruised heart doesn't suffer further." He yanked her across the carriage and onto his lap. "But, *cara*, you need to know I've never wanted anyone as much as I want you. If you need time to accept what I already know, I can give it to you."

His announcement terrified her. Could she have faith he meant what he said? She wanted to believe him. Give in to the desire, the deep seated need, to belong to him. The idea of it though—if he left her again, she'd never recover. It was too big of a risk. She couldn't trust him with her heart.

"I don't want anything from you." She wiggled in his arms. "Let me go."

"I can promise you forever." He caressed her cheek and brushed a wayward curl behind her ear. "Letting you go is not an option I can entertain."

"Nothing is forever, including this sudden desire to have me."

She had to get out of his arms. The feelings he created inside of her—she wouldn't be able to control her desires if she remained on his lap. He made her want—no, need—him and only him. Damian couldn't know how much she craved his love. Only he made her feel this deep yearning for more.

"What I feel for you, *cara*, is so far from sudden it is ridiculous to even suggest it."

"Then where have you been?" She raised an eyebrow. "Not here with me. So don't attempt to make me believe you've been fighting your feelings and desires for me. I'm not a fool."

"It couldn't be helped—I..."

She shook her head, and interrupted him, "It don't want to hear your excuses." She placed her hands on his chest to push him away, but got lost in the sensation of feeling his warmth beneath them. "Stay away from me. It's all I need from you. I can't say it enough to make you understand."

"I will give you anything you want, anything but that." His gaze softened as he stared into her eyes. "I need you too much. When you're ready to know why I've been away, I'll explain it. In the meantime, I think I should remind you exactly what is between us."

He pulled her closer and placed his lips softly upon hers. Pearla started to pull away but then lost herself in the sensation of his lips against her, and the passion she'd been trying to hold in. His caresses soothed her wounded soul. She wanted to believe everything he was trying to put into that one kiss, but it was all too much. She was on an emotional overload that threatened to burst her at the seams. The kiss went on forever and wrecked her from the inside out. She shook with a need she couldn't describe. Fear took a hold of her and she yanked her head back.

"You shouldn't have done that." Her breathing was ragged. "Release me."

He complied with her request. His arms slackened and he set her on the seat next to him. The carriage came to an abrupt halt, causing her to fall back into his arms once again. She peeked up at him through hooded eyes. She could see retrained desire deep in his silver pools.

"I believe we've reached our destination, *cara*." He smoothed another loose curl behind her ear. "This is where we part—for now. I'll call upon you in a few days. I think you need some time to think." He smiled, softly. "But rest assured, this is not over."

He caressed her cheek once more and left her alone in the carriage. Her hand flew to where the warmth from his hand was still imprinted upon her cheek. She couldn't help the need to absorb it all deep inside of her. Damian was a force that was hard to resist.

How was she supposed to argue against him when he left her an emotional wreck? Already he was beginning to break down every one of her walls of defense. If he came at her full force, it wouldn't take long to crumble them all to the ground. Damian had thrown the first volley in their war, and it looked like he planned a siege that would outlast any resistance she had to offer.

The only question she had was—why was she fighting at all?

CHAPTER TEN

*D*amian scanned the room, looking for the only person he wanted to socialize with. When he didn't see her pretty blonde head he decided to head toward the card room. He would find entertainment elsewhere while he waited for Pearla to arrive. He had it on good authority she planned on attending the Silverton ball. Arturo had someone installed in her household to garner the information he needed to court her properly.

Pearla was being difficult.

She had managed to evade him for a whole fortnight. When she'd claimed to want him to leave her be, she'd not been lying. He hadn't believed for a moment that was what she truly wanted or needed.

DAWN BROWER

The way she reacted to their kiss suggested she desired him as much as he did her.

She was afraid. If he was patient enough, he would get her to agree to be his wife in truth. He still thought of her as his. At first, he balked at the idea of taking a wife, but now that he'd gotten over his initial reservations he saw that only Pearla would do for him. She was his equal in every way. He couldn't wait for her to see it as clearly as he did.

"Didn't expect to run into you here," a voice said from behind him.

"Hello, Noah." Damian smiled. "I didn't think I'd see you not permanently attached to my sister's side."

Noah laughed and clapped his hand against Damian's shoulder. "As much as I'd enjoy that, she'd kill me if I tried. She demands her space. Gemma and Lily currently have her full attention. I expect Liam and Rand to join me in here shortly. Once the ladies get talking, they tend to ignore us."

The other two men could provide a decent distraction for him while he awaited Pearla's arrival. She was the only reason he'd ventured to the ball at all. They were not his usual scene. Thanks to his sister's social status, he got invited to all the big social events of the season, but most of the time he

130

declined them. There were too many mamas seeking to marry their daughters to him. As far as he was concerned, he was officially off the market—if he'd ever been on it at all. It was Pearla or none.

"Then we have enough for our own game." Damian grinned. "Why don't we make it interesting."

"I'm all for something interesting?" Liam asked.

Rand followed in close behind him and said, "Please, nothing too exciting. The last time you kept things from me we had to rescue our wives from a mad man. I'd like something a little less stimulating."

There was a story there. Damian would ask about it later. If he were to guess, it probably had something to do with Paolo. Why would he have kidnapped all three women? There were some things Arturo hadn't told him.

Liam rolled his eyes. "We didn't intend for them to be taken. How many times do we have to apologize for that mess?"

"For the rest of your miserable life," Rand quipped. "If you'd let me know what was going on, maybe I could have kept Lily home."

Noah snorted. "What delusional world are you living in? You do know your wife is one of the stubbornest women to ever been born, right?"

Damian hid a smile. He missed this. He didn't

know Rand well, but he hoped to become good friends with him. Liam and Noah were best friends, and included him whenever he visited his sister. Rubina marrying Noah had been one of the best things to happen to her—and him. It gave them more of a family. They had their father, but no one else.

Rand narrowed his eyes and glared at Noah. "Watch how you're speaking about Lily. She'd the epitome of everything that is wonderful, and I'll not have you impugning upon her sparkling reputation."

Liam laughed and clutched his chest. "I love Lily. I do. She is my sister after all… But, Rand, you are being a bit blind to her faults."

"No more than you or Noah regarding your own wives."

"He does have a point, gentleman," Damian interrupted. "How do you feel about a game of cards?"

They all turned toward him and nodded. Each of them pulled a chair out and sat around the table. Damian was glad he'd ventured out of his rooms. The evening looked to be entertaining already. Once Pearla came, he could claim a dance—or three, and begin to convince her they belonged together. In the meantime, a rowdy good card game would hold his attention.

Liam shuffled the cards and dealt them to each player. He looked across the table and asked Damian, "So, are you going to finally get around to telling us where you've been for the past couple of years?"

Damian sighed. He knew at some point he would have to explain what Paolo had to done him. He didn't want to relive the experience. It had been hell for too long. He was finally free, and all he wanted to do was forget the horror he'd endured. It was time to move forward with his life. Living in the past was not on his agenda.

"I hadn't planned on talking about it at all," he explained.

"Rubina isn't going to let you get away with that. You might as well practice with us. Tell us the grue-some details so we can keep them from our wives' innocent ears." Noah picked up his cards and sorted them. "You know you can tell us anything. We won't judge."

Noah, Rand, and Liam were not going to allow him keep his secrets. If he let them, they'd pull every single one. Maybe he should talk about it. Then the men would leave him alone.

"There isn't much to tell." He didn't glance up from his cards. Damian knew if he did, he'd see their gazes trained on him, awaiting his response. He didn't want to see pity in their eyes. "Paolo arranged for me to serve an indenture on an island of hell."

Dead silence.

He glanced up and didn't quite observe what he thought he would. No sympathy for what had happened to him. What he saw was more on the brink of intense rage about to explode.

"What exactly did you have to do on this island?" Liam asked, quietly.

"I don't really want to discuss it. The good news is I'm no longer there. I have a friend that helped me escape. He's on his way home to his family in India. If not for Hian, I might not have survived. I owe him my life."

"Fair enough," Noah agreed. "Why don't you explain what Pearla had to do with any of it." This was something different entirely. Damian expected Noah to be protective of her. It only surprised him it had taken him this long to broach the subject.

"Pearla had nothing to do with my indenture." Damian flipped a card onto the table. "She is the only good thing that has happened to me in the past couple of years."

Noah set his cards down and studied him. He didn't say a word for several seconds. They seemed to tick off in his head with a steady beat of uncertainty. He had no clue what was going on through the duke's head.

"How did you two meet?" He folded his arms across his chest. "I wasn't aware you two had been introduced."

Damian tossed his cards on the table. This game had taken a different turn. The men had lost interest as they sought details on his misfortune. The only way to get them to leave it be was to tell them everything. He scrubbed his hands across his face and took a deep breath. "It's a long story, and you're not going to like any of it."

"Start from the beginning," Noah offered. "It's usually a good place for a story to unfold from."

Damian nodded. He told him about Captain Blythe—what Pearla believed was their phony wedding ceremony, and finished with his indenture. He left out some details. Like the hot sun, his often burned skin, along with the bruises and cuts he suffered daily. The long hours and the malnourishment topped the list of evil he had to endure, but were not the worst for him. The belief that Pearla needed him is what kept him going. He'd had to find the strength to survive and find her. Now that he had, she didn't want him around. A part of him was devastated to hear her harsh words. He wouldn't give up on her. Thinking of her every night saved his life, and he believed they were meant to be together. It would take a little longer to convince her of it as well.

"What are you going to do?" Rand asked. "Speaking from experience—a stubborn woman is going to run fast and as far as possible before she admits she wants to be with you."

Liam snorted. "I thought my sister was the epitome of all that as wonderful in the world."

"And she is." He grinned. "But despite what you think, I am aware of every one of her faults. If we'd not been forced to spend time on a ship for weeks, she would have never sat still long enough for me to court her. Damian here is at a disadvantage. Pearla isn't afraid to travel the world to flee his presence."

"Thanks, man. That is all the encouragement I needed," Damian said, blandly. "I'm so glad we took the time to discuss this. It's been extraordinarily useful."

Noah shook his head. "Rand has a point. Our women, and yeah, I'm including Pearla because I have no doubt you'll be able to convince her you two belong together, are incredibly obstinate. You need a plan, and lucky for you we are willing to help you devise one."

Damian smiled. These men were allies he never thought he would have in his life. He was blessed to have them, and soon he would have Pearla too. His patience was running thin. He hadn't seen her in far too long. It was time to seek her out and start his campaign to win her. Her retreat was about to end for good. You couldn't win a war if you didn't have any battles to fight.

"Thanks for the offer, but I already have one I've put into motion." Damian tapped his fingers together. "Although I might need your assistance with one thing, Noah."

"Tell me what you need and it's yours." Noah sat back in his chair and folded his arms across his chest. "I'd like to see Pearla happy, and there isn't much I wouldn't do for her."

Everything was starting to fall into place, except for the minor detail of Pearla ignoring him. He had every bit of faith he'd see her come around to his way of thinking though. He needed a bit of time to convince her that she could trust him. He had no doubts and soon neither would she.

Liam grinned. "Pearla doesn't know what's about fall at her feet, does she?"

No, she didn't, but she was about to find out. He pushed his chair back and stood. "This game has been fun, but I have a lady I need to seek out. We should do this again soon."

"Good luck," Noah replied. "You're going to need it."

"I don't need luck." Damian wiggled his eyebrows. "I have my charm, and she's already succumbed to it on more than one occasion. It's only a matter of time before she caves for good."

Their laughter followed him as he exited the card room. He needed to locate the blonde goddess that had snared his attention two years ago. She was about to realize Damian fought for what he wanted, and Pearla was a woman worth fighting for.

He weeded his way through the haute ton and stopped when he saw her. She stood with her friends: Lily, Gemma, and his sister, Rubina. She was stunning. Her golden hair was wound on her head into a perfect chignon, a few curls falling loose around her shoulders. Her gown was a sapphire blue that matched her eyes. He could close his eyes and picture the jewel tone gazing up at him. Now he had to convince her she wanted to dance the next waltz with him. He narrowed the distance between them and stopped in front of her. Her gaze met his as a weary smile formed on her face.

"Damian," Rubina said, excitedly, "I'm so glad to

see you. I expected you would come by and tell me where you've been all this time."

Damian hugged his sister. "I'm sorry I've been so remiss. I've been occupied with getting my affairs in order. I will pay call soon."

She pouted. "Is that your way of saying this isn't the place to discuss it?"

Damian barely held back a smile. His sister was relentless. He would have to make sure to visit her, or she'd come looking for him.

"Yes, Rue, it is."

"Have you seen my husband?" Gemma asked, clutching her stomach with one of her hands. "I need to leave."

"I have," Damian said. "He is in the card room with Noah and Rand."

She nodded and headed toward the room he'd just left. Gemma Marsden didn't look well. Her face was devoid of all color. Liam would take care of her. Damian wouldn't worry about her welfare. There was another lady that had his full attention.

"I think we should follow after her," Lily stated. "It might be a good time for us all to leave."

"I agree." Rubina nodded. "Damian, don't forget to come see me."

Lily and Rubina followed after Gemma. Pearla

had been doing her best to pretend he wasn't near. Her face was soft pink, and her eyes darted in every direction—avoiding looking at him directly. Damian wasn't fooled. Her cheeks were rosy with desire. When she started to follow after the other ladies, he stepped in front of her.

"Hello, *cara*. Dance with me." He didn't give her a chance to decline. He led her to the dance floor as the strands of the waltz filled his ears. It was perfect.

CHAPTER ELEVEN

*P*earla basked in the warmth of Damian's arms. She'd tried to escape before he'd led her out to the dance floor, but he was faster than she was. The last thing she wanted was to give the ton something else to talk about. If she'd outright snubbed him, it would have been food for the gossipmongers. Just a dance might be overlooked—though even that took things further than she wished to go. She wouldn't even be at the Silverton ball if Gemma hadn't insisted. Her friend meant well.

She sighed. "What game are you playing now?"

"I promise you, *cara*, you are nothing I would trifle with. You're important to me."

She couldn't trust he meant it. Her bruised heart

wouldn't survive another blow. He made her weak, and she never wanted to be weak for another man again. His transgressions were perhaps worse than Noah's had been. She could forgive the duke. How was he to know the love of his life was still alive? Now she could look back and be happy for them. They had a wonderful family and Noah smiled frequently. It was a side of him she'd not seen before.

"I wish I could believe you." She truly did. "But I can't."

Damian led her though the steps of the dance. Each one brought them a little closer together. He was maneuvering her where he wanted her to be, fully encased in his arms. The small distance the dance allowed apparently wasn't enough for him. She couldn't fault him, at least not completely. There was a part of her that wanted to be as close to him as possible and breathe his alluring scent. To be lost in everything that was this man—could be intoxicating.

Her heart beat faster as she stared up into his silver eyes. It warred with many varied emotions, many of which she didn't know if she'd be able to continue denying him. She wanted to cave and let him lead her down the decadent path his gaze promised her. Just once she wanted to lose herself and not think about what consequences lay ahead of her. If only she was a different person, in a different place, she'd fall into his arms and not look back. Sadly, she couldn't allow any of it. She'd drown in the emotional overload and crash into a mess of denial afterward.

"What will it take to convince you we belong together?" He rubbed his thumb across her hand leaving a trail of heat in its wake. "I'll do anything. Tell me what you need from me, and it's yours."

His gaze pleaded with her—twin pools of molten silver. Her resolve was beginning to shatter. Soon all the walls she erected would tumble down around her. She needed fortification. Something, anything, to keep her from falling all over again for this charismatic man...

"I can't..." She was at a loss for words.

The strands of the waltz came to a winding halt. He smiled down at her and led her off the dance floor. Damian let go of her arm at the edge of the ballroom, near the balcony. He bowed to her. "Perhaps you would consider a stroll outside."

She could use a breath of fresh air. The cool air might also help her overheated skin. Being near Damian always warmed her from the inside out. He made her feel...more than anyone ever had.

"Damian, love, it's so good to see you."

Pearla turned. A woman with midnight hair and emerald eyes approached them. Her gown was the same jewel tone as her stunning eyes. She kept moving forward until she was almost on top of Damian. An exaggeration, but Pearla wanted to push her away. She was too close, too beautiful, too every-thing, and it made her feel inferior in comparison. Who was she and why was she overly familiar with him?

Damian's jaw clenched. "Camellia, it's been a while."

"Too long." She pouted. "Where have you been? I've missed you so."

Camellia rubbed his forearm with her ungloved hand and batted her eyelashes at him. Damian gazed down at her through hooded eyes. "I think you know exactly where I've been. When did you get back? I heard you'd made an unexpected trip."

"If I'd know you were looking for me, I'd have stayed in London." She licked her plump lips and smiled coyly. "Now that I've returned, you can pay a call whenever you like. For you, I'm always available."

Pearla clenched her teeth. This is what he did with his spare time? He visited this...this...harlot? To think she'd been about to give in and tell him she wanted him too. Thank heavens she'd not said those words. He could keep company with his mistress. Pearla was done with him. Tears threatened to spill from the corner of her eyes. She had to put some distance between her and Damian before they fell down her cheeks in truth. She would not let him know how much he hurt her. As far as she was concerned, he could go to hell.

"Pardon me," she said, sarcastically. "I'll let you two get reacquainted."

"Pearla, wait…"

She spun on her heels to leave. She could hear Damian call out to her, but she ignored him. The Devil belonged with his lover. Pearla was just a challenge. A woman who denied him and he couldn't have that. Too bad. She wasn't a prize for him to add to his conquests.

The balcony called to her. She needed the cool night air for an entirely different reason. Heat coursed through her body, different than what she felt in Damian's arms. This heat was full of anger and humiliation.

"I thought I saw you inside," a voice called to her. "I was beginning to think I'd never see you again."

Pearla turned. Lord Addison was heading toward her. She frowned and shook her head. When she left

Damian, she'd wanted peace, but mostly she wanted to be alone. Lord Addison was the last person she'd expected to see. She'd been avoiding him with as much fervor as she'd ignored Damian. Neither man wanted what was best for her. They both saw her as something they needed to acquire. A trophy to put on a shelf and admire, but not really know or understand.

She curtsied. "Lord Addison. It's good to see you." It wasn't, and she stopped short of rolling her eyes. "I trust you're well?"

"I am." He nodded. "Who was that gentleman I saw you dancing with."

His mouth formed a flat, white line. He didn't like the idea of her dancing with Damian. She looked away so he wouldn't see the disdain in her eyes. Lord Addison didn't have a right to be upset she danced with another man. He had no claims on her other than the ones in his own mind. She belonged to no one and could dance with whomever she pleased.

"Conte Leone is well respected."

"Is he?" He sounded uncertain. "I don't know him."

She spun around and smiled. "He's the Duchess of Huntly's brother."

"Isn't she…" He turned toward the ballroom and

then back to her. "I mean to say, weren't you engaged to the Duke of Huntly?"

Why did he have to sound so intrigued at the connection? More importantly, why couldn't the blasted man leave her alone? She had to get away from him. Only then would she obtain the peace she desired. Pearla gazed up at him and fixed a serene smile on her face. She could get through this. She needed to remember to breathe. "Yes, I was."

His frown was one of disapproval. It was all over his face in the moonlight. "Why are you associating with them? They are not worthy of you. He left you at the altar."

Was he serious? She rolled her eyes. He had to be the most ridiculous man she'd ever met. "He didn't have a choice. Rubina is his wife. Do you think he should have married me when he already was? Tell me how that makes sense?"

"Of course not," his voice was full of disdain. "It doesn't discount the fact he dishonored you."

Pearla blew out a breath of frustration. There was no reasoning with Lord Addison, so she wasn't going to waste her time. She'd much rather go home and curl up in her warm bed. Maybe she should get a pet. They were at least loyal and didn't feel the need to dictate to her. First thing in the morning, she'd look into acquiring a dog.

"Right, of course." She paused and smiled brightly. Her cheeks burned with the effort of holding the false grin in place. "But I quite like spending time with my friends, so I've chosen to let the past go. Since *I* am the one that was slighted, I feel it is within my power to forgive and openly socialize with whomever I wish to."

She hoped she'd gotten the message across loud and clear. There wasn't a chance in hell she'd stop calling on her friends because Lord Addison disapproved. She'd rather poke her eyes out with a hot needle than try to please him. He seemed like a nice enough man, even if he was rather bossy... That didn't mean she wanted to spend the rest of her days in his company.

He moved closer to her and bent his head to stare into her eyes. "You're correct. It is the sign of a graceful and generous person to forgive."

She mentally rolled her eyes. So glad he approved. "It was nice to see you again, but I am going to go home. It's been a rather tedious evening, and I feel a megrim coming on."

Pearla moved around him to head back inside. He grabbed her wrist, halting her progress.

"Wait," he demanded. "I wasn't done speaking with you."

She stared up at him, anger spiking through her once again. "That may be, but I was finished with our conversation. Let me go."

His grip tightened around her arm causing a sharp pain to travel through her hand. She winced as the pain increased as he continued to squeeze her wrist. Lord Addison yanked her closer to him. "Why are you always in a hurry to leave me? Don't you understand I hold you in the highest esteem?"

"You're hurting me." Pearla tried to wrench her wrist from within his firm hold.

He lifted his other arm and skimmed his fingers across her hair. She shuddered and jerked her head. "You're so beautiful, Miss Montgomery."

"Am I interrupting?" Damian strolled out to the balcony. His gait was elegant and unaffected. He appeared to not have a care in the world.

"Yes, you are." Lord Addison seethed.

"I don't think I am." Damian studied him. "Pearla, would you like to go back inside with me?"

She yanked her arm free at last and rubbed her tender wrist. "Indeed, I would. Good evening, Lord Addison," Pearla said with disdain. She spun on her heels and let Damian lead her back inside.

"Was he forcing his intentions on you?"

She was glad Damian had come to her rescue. That didn't mean she was going to encourage him. It hadn't been that long since she was trying to escape him and his arranged tryst with the lovely Camellia. Instead of answering him, she remained silent for their entire trek inside. She nodded to members of the ton as she passed them, leaving a smile on her face as she walked. When they reached the far end of the ballroom near the exit she stopped in her tracks and turned to him. "Thank you for the escort, but I'm going to have to bid you farewell now."

"Don't be so quick to run away, *cara*." He rubbed her tender wrist with intense gentleness. A red welt appeared where Lord Addison had gripped it. "I know he hurt you. He will pay for that."

Anger spiked her blood hot. "I don't need you to fight all my battles for me, Damian. Go find your mistress and spend the evening with her. I will be fine. I'm more than capable of seeing myself home."

He smiled. Why did he have to be so devastatingly handsome? Damn man. She wanted to smack the cocky grin right off his perfect face. That was what bothered her the most. He had looked even better standing next to the flawless Camellia. She ached deep down to the edge of her soul and feared a part of her would forever want this man.

"I assure you, I do not have, nor do I want, a mistress."

She raised an eyebrow and considered throwing the woman and their little tête-à-tête back at him, but held back the retort. Throwing insults and trading innuendos with Daman was counterproductive to what she wanted.

"It matters not. I am going home." She shrugged. "What you do with your time is your business."

He chuckled. "Sweetness, I do believe you're jealous."

She opened her mouth as shock filled her. He was *right*. She *was*. Not that she would ever admit to such a lowly emotion. Damian didn't deserve to know how she felt about him. It was bad enough she was privy to it on a daily basis.

"I wouldn't deign to give you the pleasure."

"Oh, darling," he coaxed. "I promise you one day I will show you so much bliss you won't doubt where my affection lies."

He was trying to tempt her again. She couldn't give in. This conversation had to end before she did the unthinkable and fell willingly into his embrace.

She had to be strong and remember who he really was. Damian was not the man for her—no man was.

"Good bye, Damian."

She turned on her heels and took slow steady steps to put distance between them. It wouldn't do for him to realize she was running away from him, and as fast as possible to save face.

"You can run, Pearla." His laugher floated up to her ears. "But you can't hide. We will be seeing each other again soon. And, *cara,* that's a promise you can count on."

She gritted her teeth. So much for pretending she wasn't trying to escape him and the allure he held for her… It was silly of her to think she'd fooled him for even a second. Damian appeared to have the ability to see right through her—and it scared her senseless.

CHAPTER TWELVE

*D*amian watched Pearla as she left the ball. He was willing to let her leave because he knew one of his men would follow her and ensure she made it home safely. With her gone, he could take care of some other important matters. They were not more important that Pearla, but still had to be dealt with. First, he had to track down Lord Addison and inform him he was never to go near her again. Pearla had played it down, but the man had hurt her. What Lord Addison had hoped to accomplish, Damian did not know. Before he left the Silverton Ball, he would beat the answers out of him, if necessary. He really hoped the man proved difficult. He was bloody pissed off anyone had dared to hurt the woman he loved.

He stalked toward the last place he'd saw the cur. After scanning the area, his gaze landed on Lord Addison as he left the ballroom. Where was he going? It didn't matter. It gave him the opportunity to have a conversation with him in private. He didn't want word to get back to Pearla he'd pummeled the man after she departed. That was one thing he would keep to himself. He didn't want to worry her. This was something he'd gladly handle. Lord Addison would not bother her ever again.

"A word if you will, Lord Addison." He followed him inside the library and shut the door with a soft click. He stalked forward until he was directly in front of him. "I believe we have a few things to discuss."

Lord Addison turned his nose up at him. "I can't fathom what."

The more he was around the man, he liked him even less. "No?" He raised an eyebrow. "Why don't we being with your intentions toward Miss Montgomery."

As in, he wouldn't have any after he was done with him. The bastard was going to forget she existed. His jaw tightened as he studied Lord Addison. The man appeared completely unruffled in his presence. Did he really believe he was safe? Did he not know what Damian was capable of?

"My intentions are honorable of course," he replied. "Though I fail to see how it is any concern of yours, but I intend to marry her."

Never mind beating him senseless. Lord Addison needed to die. The sooner he stopped breathing, the easier it would be for Damian to relax.

"She's not interested." He clenched his teeth together into a snarl. "You're to leave her alone and not bother her any further with unwanted attention."

Lord Addison laughed. "That's a good one. You're playing a joke on me, correct?" He paused and stared at Damian. "Oh, I see. You're serious. Why would I cease to court her? Miss Montgomery has not indicated she was averse to my suit."

Damian clenched his fists against his side. It wasn't time yet. Just a little bit longer and he could wipe the satisfied smirk off of Lord Addison's face. When he was done with the lord, he would know exactly who Pearla belonged to.

"You don't need to hear anything from Miss Montgomery. She wasn't too happy with you outside on the balcony. You left bruises on her wrist." Damian took two even steps closer to him. "A man with honorable intentions doesn't hurt a woman in his care." He'd pay it back tenfold. He'd be throbbing with pain much stronger than Pearla currently was.

Lord Addison stared at Damian and gulped. He finally realized he was in a room alone with an enraged beast. If he didn't tread carefully, he would be shredded. Damian grinned evilly. It was about time he realized the danger he courted by hurting Pearla.

Damian took two more steps. Lord Addison retreated.

"Can we remain civilized?"

"No," Damian replied. "I believe we've passed the very idea of it the moment you thought you had the right to touch her."

He yanked him by his cravat and lifted him off the ground. A little swine of a man, barely worth the effort to warn off, but for Pearla, Damian would do anything. Even send Lord Addison to hell where he belonged. Maybe that was even too good for him. Perhaps he should put the sod on ship to visit a different kind of hell.

"Tell me, Lord Addison, have you ever had the opportunity to travel?"

"Um, I had a world tour…" He was shaking in his

grasp. "And I returned from France a short time ago."

Damian laughed. "What about Fiji?" The living hell he'd left might be a good place to send Lord Addison.

"I—I," he stuttered. "Please, release me."

"You mean the same way you were going to let go of Pearla's wrist earlier?" He tilted his head and studied the man. "You're right, I should give you the same consideration."

Damian squeezed his neck until he started to turn purple, and then punched him in his stomach. After he let him go, Lord Addison fell to the floor with a loud thud. He gasped for breath and tore his cravat off.

"You—why—I don't understand," he gasped out.

"I don't intend to kill you. I never did, and as much as I'd like to send you to hell so you'll never bother my intended again, I can't do that. It would make me no better than you." Damian leaned down and said with conviction, "But rest assured if you ever go near her again, I will, and I won't think twice about it. She is mine to protect now."

He scooted backward. "I didn't know—Miss Montgomery never said..."

That didn't surprise him. He had yet to win her

over. Soon the whole world would know she was his. He could be patient for her to accept it. This man didn't need to know more than she belonged to him.

"She shouldn't have to say anything to be respected. Leave before I change my mind."

Lord Addison raced out of the library. Damian scanned the room. His eyes locked onto a brandy decanter and decided he needed—no, deserved—a drink. He understood Pearla's reluctance, but it was playing havoc on him. What he needed was to be able to shout from the rooftops she was his. This cloak and dagger routine was getting old. He poured brandy into a glass and then downed the contents in one gulp. It burned as it traveled down his throat.

Clapping echoed through the room. "That was quite the performance. I must thank you for the entertainment."

Damian spun and locked gazes with Captain Blythe. It appeared to be his lucky night. The other man he needed to have words with had walked back into his life.

"Ah, Captain, good to see you. I've been looking for you."

"I heard," he replied. "I have my own spies too."

Damian poured another glass of brandy and took

a slow drink. "I wouldn't expect less from someone employed by the late Duca d'Sordillo. I'm only surprised it's taken you this long to track me down."

"Be a good sport and pour me a glass of that brandy. I think we have a few things we must iron out."

Damian didn't want to have a lengthy conversation with the man. He wanted a few quick answers. The fight had left him when Lord Addison scurried out of the room. Now, he wanted to go home and plot how to win Pearla's heart for good.

"Pour your own brandy. I'm not your servant." Damian gestured toward the decanter. "As far as working through a few things… Tell me one thing, and we can be done with each other."

He raised an eyebrow. "What is it you want to know?"

"Why did you marry us?"

He didn't ask if the marriage was valid. It didn't matter anymore. Damian had no problem going through another ceremony. Pearla would never believe that the marriage was real without one. If it alleviated her concerns, then he'd do it a thousand times—as long as the end result was the same. She'd be his forever.

"I assume you're speaking about Miss Montgomery." He grinned. "I did enjoy watching, or rather hearing, you defending her honor."

Damian took a deep breath and glared at the Captain. "Are you going to explain what your master plan was?"

He shrugged and headed toward the brandy decanter. The Captain poured himself a glass and took a sip. He took his time before he turned back to Damian.

"It seemed like a good idea at the time."

That was it? Damian didn't buy it. There had to be more to his motivation than a spur of the moment idea. "I don't believe you."

He laughed and explained, "Conte, I'm not obsessed with you like the Fonte family is. I was— bored. The two of you amused me. I thought if I married you, it would prove to be rather entertaining. I admit that the duca thought that it would be good fun to ruin Miss Montgomery and you be the one who accomplished the task." The captain shrugged. "He believed the Duke of Huntly would never forgive you for ruining his former intended."

Damian clenched his jaw. "He would have destroyed an innocent woman's life to tamper with my relationship with Noah?"

"There isn't anything that the duca wouldn't have

done." He swallowed the contents of his glass and set it down. "You were a pawn in a much larger scheme."

What Captain Blythe was telling him proved interesting, but it didn't really answer his questions. He needed to understand it fully in order to move forward. "Care to explain what his plans entailed?"

"No," he paused and studied Damian, "As fun as this has been, I think I've told you all I can."

"You haven't told me anything at all. This conversation is leaving me with even more questions and no answers to speak of."

Captain Blythe shrugged and headed toward the door. He paused before exiting and turned back to Damian. "There's not much I can do about that. The duca was only one boss in a crowd of many, and I rather like my head attached to my body. If I say any more, I might not keep it there."

Damian gritted his teeth and clenched his hand into a tight fist. The more he talked, the more he wanted to plant a fist into his face. If he wasn't going to depart with useful information regarding Paolo and his cohorts, then he could at least tell him something else of import.

"Before you scamper off," Damian said. "Why does Pearla believe we are not actually married?"

His laugh filled the room, making Damian want

to act on his impulses. "I'm afraid that is my fault." He shrugged. "I told you I was suffering from ennui. After we took you away and deposited you on that infernal island, I decided she didn't need to mourn your loss. I gave her a reason to be angry with you instead —after all, no one intended for you to leave Fiji and see her ever again. She needed to move on with her life. Perhaps find someone worthy of her. She is a rather lovely woman."

Damian enunciated each word, barely holding in his rage. "What. Did. You. Tell. Her."

"I simply explained how you were only using her." He shrugged. "That you hoped to entice her into your bed and help her lose her virtue along the way."

"What does that have to do with our marriage?" No wonder she was so reluctant to be with him. The Captain had done them a tremendous disservice.

"Oh, that. I explained how it wasn't valid, and only a tool to get you what you really desired from her." He grinned. "There was also the little bit about how you were in on the plan from the start. The lady wasn't amused."

Damian cursed. "So it's true. Our wedding was a hoax to entertain you on the voyage to rid the world of me?"

"Yes," Captain Blythe said and left the room.

Damian threw his half-filled glass and watched it shatter against the wall. The amber liquid dripped down and hit the floor. It still didn't assuage the rage burning inside , so he turned and punched the wall, cursing from the pain shooting through him. How was he going to win Pearla back when she believed the worst of him? At least he knew what poison Captain Blythe had filled her head with. He would have to show her with his actions how much she meant to him. No matter how much he told her he wanted her, she wouldn't truly believe it. Not when he'd been forced to leave her before and she'd felt abandoned, as well as used.

He had an uphill battle from the moment he'd been torn from her side. In the end, he would prevail. The beginnings of love had been stamped in her heart. All he had to do was remind her of the man she'd trusted with her tender heart.

Damian smiled. *Soon, cara, soon I will begin to unlock your deepest desires.*

CHAPTER THIRTEEN

*P*earla sat across from Gemma and Lily in the carriage as they headed to the Huntly townhouse. She'd stopped by, and her friends had talked her into a visit with Rubina. The last time she'd called upon the duchess—if it could be called that—was when she'd renewed her wedding vows with Noah. She still didn't know why she had attended the ceremony. Gemma thought it would be a good idea. What had she called it? Oh yeah, closure. It had been good for her to see how much in love the couple was. Though it made her ache for something similar.

"What is going on inside that head of yours?" Gemma asked.

"Hmmm," Pearla said absently.

"Pearla," Lily exclaimed.

She turned toward them and stared, baffled. What had they been saying? She'd been lost in her own world. There was too much on her mind and she had no idea how to deal with it all. When she'd seen Damian with Camellia the night before, her heart had hurt even more than before. It shouldn't matter that he had a mistress. They were nothing to each other. As much as she pushed him away, she couldn't help how much she desired him. Pushing him away was the only way she could continue to protect herself.

"Yes?" she asked, raising an eyebrow. "What?"

Lily and Gemma exchanged a look. What did that mean?

"I told you," Gemma said.

Lily chuckled. "You did."

Pearla rolled her eyes. "All right, I'll ask. What did you tell her?"

She didn't have the patience to play guessing games with her two friends. In fact, she lacked any tolerance what-so-ever. Her temper was at an all-time high, and she'd been snapping for no reason at all. The staff tiptoed around her.

Lily smiled. "You have something, or should I say someone, on your mind. Do you care to share?"

"I have nothing on my mind." Only one handsomely wicked conte that wouldn't leave her thoughts no matter how much she tried. "Nothing of import. I was thinking perhaps it would be lovely to have a dinner party. Would you two be willing to come?"

The last thing she wanted was a dinner party, but she needed to distract them in some way. She could get through an entire evening of their company if it halted the current conversation.

Gemma shook her head. "You're not getting off that easy."

Lily nodded. "We know something is bothering you, and you're going to tell us. If you want to discuss dinner plans, we will do so afterward."

"Why are you two being so difficult?" Pearla sighed. "I don't wish to discuss it."

"Don't you think it's time?" Gemma asked, softly.

Pearla resisted the urge to stomp her foot and throw a tantrum that would put a two-year-old to shame. How many times must she tell them? She only had one wish—to forget Damian Leone existed. All he'd done was destroy any chance she'd love another man. She'd thought she loved Noah. She hadn't realized how bland her emotions were for the duke until she met the conte. Now when she closed her eyes all she saw was his silver eyes alight with passion.

"I rather not." She turned her head away so they couldn't see the fear in her eyes.

"Tell us what happened with Damian," Lily insisted. "We know there is a story there. He claimed you were his wife when he interrupted the wedding."

The carriage came to a screeching halt, giving her a reprieve. Pearla took the opportunity to exit the carriage and head to the front door. Surely they wouldn't discuss the duchess's brother in her presence. She could pretend the conversation hadn't turned around and cornered her.

"Don't think this is over with," Gemma said from behind her. "It's only paused for a few moments."

Drat. So much for thinking they'd drop it around Rubina. Pearla sighed. "Why won't you leave it be?"

"Because we can see your heart in your eyes whenever he's around. It's time to face your problems head-on. If you want him, and we think you do, we are going to do whatever we can to make sure you get him." Lily patted her on the hand. "I have experience here. So does Gemma. Let us do this for you."

They walked into the townhouse and into Rubina's sitting room. She was already waiting for them. "Good, you're here. Did you ask her?"

"Yes, we did," Gemma answered her. "And no, we don't have answers yet."

The duchess stared at them for a brief moment, and then shook her head. Pearla didn't want to know what was going through her thoughts. She was very much afraid she wouldn't like it one bit.

Rubina waved them in. "Come sit, refreshments will be here shortly."

"Did you plan this?" Pearla asked as she looked back and forth between the three women. How could they do this to her? She thought they were her friends.

"We had planned on confronting you…" Gemma began.

"But we were not going to ask you yet. You happened to make it easier for us by stopping by to see Gemma today. All we did was take advantage of the situation," Lily finished.

"They're right. I wasn't expecting you. Lily and Gemma, yes, but it is a surprise." Rubina smiled. "A welcome one, but I apologize if I've made you uncomfortable."

Pearla gulped down a lump that formed in her throat. She wanted to run away from them. Perhaps they were right and it was time to face her fears. What if she *could* have Damian? If they were aware of something that she wasn't... Perhaps he'd shared something with his sister. Did she dare ask?

She paced the room as anxiety filled her. Where should she start? "After the wedding..." She paused and took a deep breath and turned toward them. "I left."

"We know that." Lily waved her hand. "Tell us how you ended up with Damian."

Pearla glanced at each of their faces. They appeared a little too eager to hear the details. Why were they so interested in what happened? Rubina must not know much if they were all interrogating Pearla.

"I'm getting to that." Such impatience. "I booked passage on a ship. It seemed like fate, and I could get out of England and away from the embarrassment."

Rubina blushed. "I'm sorry about that—if I could have returned sooner, I would have."

Pearla waved her hand. She no longer blamed the woman. How could she? It wasn't as if she planned to hurt her. An evil man had held her captive in his home for years. She had suffered more than Pearla ever had. "I know, and there is nothing to forgive. Damian explained what happened to you. I'm sorry you had to go through so much pain. You and Noah shouldn't have been put through that because a mad man had been obsessed with you. It's clear to see how much you two love each other. I'm happy for you."

"Thank you," Rubina said quietly. Her tone was soft, yet demanding. "This would be a good place to tell us about your relationship with my brother."

"Don't skip the good parts," Lily interjected. Gemma smacked her on the shoulder. "What? Don't tell me you're not curious. I'll call you a liar."

Pearla smiled. This was a good thing. They *were* her friends, and she *could* trust them. "The Duca d'Sordillo kidnapped Damian and arranged for him to be on the ship I booked passage on."

"He implied as much, but we couldn't find the evidence we needed to confirm it. Paolo is an evil man." Rubina sighed. "We feared Damian died at his hands."

"Did you help rescue him?" Lily prodded. Gemma glared at her. "Quit giving me that look, Gemma Marsden. We've been waiting long enough to hear this story, and I don't want her to get distracted."

Gemma sighed and shook her head. "Please continue, Pearla."

Pearla laughed. "Thank you."

"For what?" Rubina asked.

Warmth spread through her. She didn't know how much she'd needed this…time with these three women to help her put it into perspective.

"For forcing me to talk about it."

She told them everything. Explained how she'd been locked in a cabin with Damian for weeks. The wedding Captain Blythe had forced on them, and then the finale when Damian had left. When she found out the wedding had been nothing but a sham, and then the captain's claims Damian had orchestrated it.

Rubina shook her head. "I don't know what happened to my brother. He hasn't bothered to explain any of it to me yet. That tells me it isn't good, or he'd have spilled all of the details already. He's always been protective of me." She frowned. "I do know this: he cares for you, and he wouldn't have left you willingly. I bet my life Captain Blythe lied to you. Talk to him and let him explain what happened."

Pearla bit her lip and considered her words. Rubina would know Damian better than anyone. Could she trust him again? She wanted to. Her heart belonged to him in a way it never had to anyone else.

If he loved her—she could have everything. But what if she did as Rubina suggested and he broke her all over again. Could she take a chance and lose everything?

"I don't know if I can…" She looked away from them. "I thought I loved Noah. I know now I didn't have a clue what love is. If I go to Damian and lay my heart before him, I don't know if I'd survive it if he tossed it aside."

"Why do you have reservations?" Gemma asked. "Has he done something to make you believe he'd hurt you?"

"Other than the lies that Captain Blythe told you," Lily said. "Because it's clear he had his own agenda."

Pearla glanced at Rubina. "Do you know a Camellia?"

Rubina's face lost all color. Her voice was high-pitched as she demanded, "How do you know *her*?"

Pearla sighed. She knew that woman was trouble. "I saw her last night at the Silverton ball. She was awfully friendly with Damian. Her words implied that they were—involved."

Please let me be wrong. She didn't like to think of Damian with another woman.

Rubina took a deep breath. "Camellia is Paolo's

younger sister." She waved her hand. "Which isn't important... Damian and Camellia were—courting I guess is the word. I know now that it was much deeper than that."

Pearla's heart broke. It was as she feared. He did have a past with the stunning woman. "I see." She fought tears. This was not the time to give into the pain.

"No, you don't," Rubina said softly. "Damian never loved her. She was a tool. He knew if he got close to her, he'd be able to find out more about Paolo's organization." She frowned. "I hate to admit this, but he used her. He knew she wanted him, and he saw it as a way to end Paolo's criminal activity."

Camellia was the mistake he'd referred to when they were being held captive together. He'd said he regretted it. Pearla tilted her head and considered the information Rubina imparted. "He doesn't love her?"

"He never did." She smiled. "I do believe he loves you. I know my brother, and he's never looked at a woman the way he does you. He may have not said it out loud, but I believe you own his heart."

How was she to use this new information? It could change everything for her—she needed to talk to Damian and figure out what future they had.

"Sometimes the biggest leap you make can give you the best rewards," Gemma explained. "If I'd given up on Liam, we wouldn't be where we are now. Trust yourself and actually listen to what he has to say."

Lily smiled at Gemma. "My brother is an arse. He never should have run from you to begin with. It's the Marsden stubbornness."

Pearla knew a little about the urge to runaway. She'd been doing it for months. Her friends were right. It was time to face her fears and talk to Damian. Making assumptions was not getting her anywhere. If he loved her... Gemma was right; the rewards would be enormous. She could finally fall into his arms and feel all that pleasure he kept promising her.

"I believe it's time I acted on your advice." Pearla smiled. "I have a lot to think about, some preparation to do."

"Maybe now is the time to organize that dinner party you mentioned earlier," Lily reminded her.

"Dinner party?" Rubina's eyebrow rose. "Did I miss something."

Gemma tapped her chin. "Perhaps it would be better if Rubina planned one instead."

They all looked at Gemma. She explained her

idea and they all agreed. As Damian's sister, she could invite him and give Pearla the perfect opportunity to find some quiet time with him. It would be both proper and private. Pearla couldn't wait now that she'd decided to give him a chance. She smiled at the thought of seeing him again. A weight lifted off her shoulders she hadn't realized she'd been carrying around. For the first time in as long as she could remember the future looked bright. All she had to do was let go of all her doubts and she could have everything she wanted.

Soon, Damian. Soon.

CHAPTER FOURTEEN

*D*amian knocked on the door to his sister's home. She'd effectively demanded he attend a dinner party she planned in the invitation she'd sent to his room. He didn't doubt it was an excuse to interrogate him. Subtlety wasn't one of Rubina's strong suits. When she wanted something she asked plainly, and it appeared as if she was done waiting for him to come to her. He didn't even know why he avoided the conversation.

She wouldn't look badly upon him. If anyone knew what an evil man Paolo was it was her. There was no reason he shouldn't have explained everything to her. He had a lot on his mind, and honestly didn't have the time. His conversation with Captain Blythe had given him a lot to think about. Now he could tie up loose ends and begin to pursue Pearla in truth. He knew what she believed, and now it was up to him to alleviate every one of her misgivings.

"Good evening, Conte Leone," the butler greeted him after he opened the door. "Everyone is meeting in the sitting room until dinner is served."

"Thank you, Simmons." Damian nodded. "How many people did my sister invite to this little party of hers?"

"It's an intimate affair," he replied. "Only close friends and family."

That could mean any number of people his sister viewed as a friend—perhaps he'd get lucky and Pearla was among her guests. She had been at their renewal ceremony. It was possible. Damian nodded at Simmons and headed to the sitting room. He found his sister engrossed in a quiet conversation with the object of his desire. No one else was in the room.

"Am I early?" he asked.

He usually was one of the last to arrive. By all appearances, he wasn't though. Who were they waiting for? A small part of him hoped no one else would be in attendance. He could easily squire Pearla away for a little heart-to-heart and finally convince her she belonged with him.

Rubina smiled brightly. "You're right on time. Come in and join us." She patted the settee. "We've much to discuss."

Dread began to pool inside of him. What had his sister planned? He raised an eyebrow. "We do?"

They'd had their heads together whispering when he'd entered. He had an uneasy feeling they were up to something. The demand for him to attend should have been a warning. His sister had no problems hatching a scheme to get what she wanted. He dreaded finding out what she was up to.

Rubina nodded. "Absolutely."

Pearla had yet to acknowledge his presence. She did great at pretending he didn't exist. Why did he think that would have changed? When he spoke to her directly, she lit up from the inside out. He forced her to admit what was between them. If he let her, she'd go on ignoring the fire burning deep inside them both.

Damian sat down next to his sister and glanced between Pearla and Rubina. Their wide grins were not very comforting; they only made him more uneasy. "Where is everyone?"

Pearla remained quiet. It was enough to give a man a complex. How could she find it so easy to ignore him? He was exceptionally aware of her whenever she was in his presence. What would it take to stir her emotions to the surface?

"Never mind about the guest list." Rubina waved her hand. "I've been talking to Pearla, and I think you have a few things to explain."

Damian glanced at Pearla again. She met his gaze with determination. He looked at his sister and encountered the same expression from her. They'd effectively lured him to a dressing down as if he was an errant school boy. He wanted to laugh, but he knew they were serious. He would play their game, and then he'd have his own private time with Pearla. He was done with the chase, and he wanted to claim her as his.

"What is it you think I need to enlighten you both with?" He leaned back into the settee and watched them both carefully.

"I have been waiting patiently for you to tell me what happened to you." Rubina glared at him. "I've been forced to ask Pearla to fill in some of the blanks. You interrupted my wedding and claimed she was your wife. Then nothing..." She waved her hand.

He could almost feel Pearla's stare burning through him. He turned and gazed into twin blue flames. She wanted to cut in but held back. This was

Rubina's show, and Pearla was waiting for her turn to pounce. He wanted her to. It was about bloody time she sought him out. It was a nice turn of events.

He tapped his fingers together. "At the time, I believed that to be true. I've since realized I was duped by someone in the employ of Paolo."

Rubina tilted her head. "There is more to it than that. What happened to you after you left Pearla on that ship with Captain Blythe?"

Ah...so Pearla had filled her in on the details she was aware of. That made things a little simpler. He still didn't want to get into the fine details of his horror as an indentured slave. No one needed to know how bad it had been. He still had nightmares about it. In time, he'd be able to let it go, but he wasn't going to subject the two most important women in his life to the atrocities he suffered. He didn't need to share his ordeal and add to their pain.

"Paolo arranged for me to spend some time on a secluded island near Australia."

Pearla's head snapped toward him. "Don't do that."

Finally, she spoke. It took her long enough. "Do what?"

"Make it seem like you were on holiday when we both know it was far more than that."

Did they? Was she finally able to see past Captain Blythe's lies? Things might have progressed far more than he realized. She seemed—open, almost trusting as she gazed at him. What caused her to finally see clearly? Still...he didn't plan on giving all the details.

He shrugged. "A lot happened, *cara*, but none of which matters. If it's all the same to you both, I'd rather forget about my time on that horrid island."

Pearla tilted her head and studied him. She was quiet for a few moments as she contemplated his words. Then, with a firm voice, she confirmed, "Captain Blythe did lie to me."

He studied her. "About some things, yes he did."

"What was a lie and what was the truth?" Pearla asked.

Rubina stood and said, "I need to check on dinner." She left the room. Damian didn't once glance in her direction. His gaze never left Pearla's. His sister had given them privacy to discuss what happened. He would thank her later for the gift.

Pearla fidgeted in her seat. She looked down at her lap. Damian wanted to ease her discomfort. The only way he knew how to do that was to tell her how much he needed her.

"I would never have willingly left you." He lifted her hand and caressed it with the pad of his thumb.

"But that wasn't his biggest lie. The one that played the most havoc on our lives was letting us both believe we'd married. It was a shock to be forced into the ceremony, but it had felt right. Now that I know it was false, all I want to do is rectify it. Please, *cara*, consent to be my wife in truth."

A soft gasp left her lips. He was afraid she might say no, so he pulled her into his arms and kissed her until he couldn't tell where she began and he ended. Not once did she try to pull away. She lifted her arms and wound them around his neck, entwining her hands in his hair. He couldn't get close enough to her. To finally have her in his arms again...no words could describe how wondrous it was. He pulled back and saw his own passion reflected back at him in her fiery gaze. This is what he'd missed and craved all the months they'd been separated. How it would be between them.

"You didn't give me a chance to answer you." Pearla cupped his cheeks. "Do you always leap without looking?"

"For you, I'd walk through hell and back."

She smiled at him. "I'm starting to believe that might be true."

His heart filled with hope. When he'd left his rooms, he never thought he'd find all his dreams waiting for him at his sister's home. Now he might finally have everything he'd been longing for. Was she telling him what he thought she was?

"Are you agreeing to marry me?" *Please say yes.* "If so, I'd like to have the ceremony as soon as possible."

"I'm still considering all my options."

His heart fell. Not the answer he'd hoped for, but still an improvement.

"What is there to consider?" He let his smile show all the pleasure he could give her. "You know what the right answer is, *cara.* Say yes, and I'll make you the happiest, most satisfied, woman in the world."

"You still haven't told me everything." She frowned. "How am I to trust you when you won't share with me what really happened to you? I know by your evasiveness it isn't good."

Not this again. Why was she being so persistent? It didn't matter the horrors he suffered. All he needed was for her to agree to spend the rest of her life in his arms. Her softness would erase the atrocities he suffered and ease his soul. "I don't wish to speak of it." He set her down on the settee and paced the room. "It isn't worth speaking about."

"Damian, please," she begged. "Make me undersand."

He ran his fingers through his hair with frustration coursing through his veins. "I was an indentured slave," he spat out. "They made me do things... I can't do this. Don't make me."

Tears trailed down her cheeks. She walked over to him and wrapped her arms around his waist, leaned her head against his chest. He closed his eyes, basking in her warmth, and held onto her with all he had inside.

"All right, you win," she muttered. "I won't push. When and if you want to talk about what you went through, I will listen."

Thank God. He enjoyed holding her. This was what he needed. To feel her wrapped in his arms. She was what he'd lived for and fought to return to. If he could keep her warmth near him forever, it would erase all the things he'd suffered on that island. None of it mattered as long as she agreed to be his. "When will you give me an answer to my question?"

She glanced up at him through hooded eyes. "I haven't made a decision."

He smiled. She was being coy now. He lifted his hand and trailed his fingers through her silky blonde hair. He pulled the pins out and let them drop to the floor one by one until her curls flowed down her back. "Perhaps I can convince you."

"Oh?" She licked her lips. "What did you have in mind?"

He kissed her forehead. "A little bit of this." He trailed kisses down her cheeks and the base of her neck. "Some more of this." His lips hovered above hers. "A whole lot of this."

He pressed his lips to hers and tasted her sweetness. Their tongues dueled for control as he pulled her tighter in his embrace. The burning flame between them threatened to set them ablaze with pleasure. Damian would never get enough of her. She was his everything.

"Dinner is…" Rubina's voice filled his ears. "Oh, um, perhaps I should come back."

Damian stepped away from Pearla and smiled. "Don't go, Rue."

"Did you two settle everything?" she asked.

"No." His gaze never left Pearla's. "I'm still waiting for her to give me an answer to my question."

"What question is that?" Noah asked as he entered the room. "What did I miss? Simmons said dinner is ready. Why are we still in the sitting room?"

Pearla's laughter filled the room. It was music to his ears.

"Please, *cara*, say the word that I have been waiting forever for you to say."

"Yes." She paused and placed a soft quick kiss on his lips. "I will marry you."

Damian hugged her tightly against him, and then glanced over his shoulder to meet Noah's gaze. He nodded, understanding what Damian was asking without words. Pearla stepped out of his embrace. A huge smile lit up her beautiful face.

Noah clapped his hands. "Great, so that special license you had me obtain will be used after all."

Pearla's gaze whipped toward Noah and back at him. She raised an eyebrow and said, "What is he talking about? You knew I'd say yes?"

"I'd never presume to know what you will or will not do, *cara*." He caressed her cheek with the palm of his hand. "I was only hoping you'd agree. On the lucky day you said yes, I wanted to be ready to say our vows all over again."

She smiled. "You were always too charming for you own good." She sighed. "So when do you want to have the ceremony?"

"After dinner."

She laughed lightheartedly. "I'm serious."

"So am I."

Pearla tilted her head and studied him. Her gaze

softened. He missed her so much and hoped she agreed to an impromptu wedding. He didn't want to give her a chance to change her mind. The sooner they had the ceremony, the happier he would be.

She shook her head and chuckled lightly. "Fine. Noah, do your magic and make it happen."

"Consider it done," he said and left the room.

Damian would owe the duke a great debt for making all his dreams come true. Soon, Pearla would be his wife, and nothing would stand in the way of their happiness.

CHAPTER FIFTEEN

*D*inner flew by in a blur. Pearla ate, but the food had no taste. Nerves filled her as she went through the motions. A vicar would be arriving soon to marry her and Damian. This time the wedding would be real.

Was she really ready to tie herself to him?

She glanced across the table, her gaze locking with his. A sense of rightness overflowed through her. *Yes.* She wanted him like she'd never wanted anything in her life. Her wedding to Noah had been planned down to the last detail, and it ended up being cancelled. This time she wasn't going to wait. Damian was hers. It was time the world knew what she already did inside her heart.

Noah sighed. "Is the food that bad?"

Pearla heard his voice, but the words hadn't registered in her mind. All she could do was stare at Damian. Waiting was killing her. She wanted to marry him and start their life together. He'd made her promises she fully intended to ensure he kept. She needed to experience the passion he guaranteed she would find in his arms.

"What?" Pearla asked absentmindedly.

Damian chuckled. "The food is fine. We're anxious to get to...*dessert*."

Pearla blushed. When he said dessert, heat permeated inside her. He hadn't meant a sweet confection when he said the word. It was much more decadent than that.

She wiped her mouth with a napkin. "Right. I am done."

"Let's retire to the sitting room." Rubina stood up. "The vicar should be here soon."

"We'll stay behind and discuss a few things." Noah gestured toward Damian. "Let us know when he arrives."

"I will." Rubina nodded. She leaned down and quickly kissed Noah. Then she wrapped her arm through Pearla's, leading her out of the room. "I'm so glad you're going to marry my brother. I've always wanted a sister."

Pearla was baffled. "Don't you find it strange?"

"What?" she asked.

"Two years ago, I was standing in a church ready to marry Noah, your husband, and now I'm about to marry your brother." Pearla didn't understand how Rubina could be so accepting of her. She didn't know if she would've been able to return the favor if their roles were reversed.

"No," Rubina said. "Everything happens for a reason. I think you were meant to be in that church so it could lead you to the one place you were destined to be."

Perhaps she was right. If she'd never fled London, she might not have fallen so quickly into Damian's arms. He'd been there when she needed someone to lean on. She'd been prickly and he'd remained charming and kind. She didn't know the full details of what happened to him when he had been torn away from her, but she hoped he would feel comfortable enough to tell her eventually. Secrets had a way of driving a wedge between people, and she didn't want to lose Damian ever again. Prying wouldn't give her the answers she sought. Only patience would do that.

"I understand." Pearla smiled. "Noah is yours, and Damian is mine. That is how it was always supposed to be, and losing Noah led me to where I really belonged."

Rubina nodded, her lips tilting into a soft smile. "These things work themselves out. I'm so glad Damian has found a woman worthy of his love."

"How do you know I am?"

Pearla bit her lip. Did he love her? He never said. Maybe that was something she should have asked him before she agreed to be his wife. They were doing everything backward. Rubina had such faith, and Pearla questioned everything. How could she believe they belonged together and would make it when Pearla constantly doubted him? One second she was sure and wouldn't change anything for any reason. Then a niggling feeling deep in her gut made her want to run away and not look back. How was such indecisiveness worthy of Damian's affection? His sister should be telling her to stay away and not break his heart.

"Now you're being silly." Rubina laughed. "You're worthy for several reasons, but the easiest and most obvious is because he loves you. That's enough for me."

There was that word again. *Love*. Rubina believed he loved Pearla. He certainly desired her and believed they belonged together. He was so gentle and possessive… *Enough*. She wasn't going to debate the merits of marrying him anymore. She'd agreed to marry him. The time for thinking about it had past.

"Pardon me, Your Grace," Simmons said. "The vicar has arrived."

"Very good. Show him in, and please let my husband and brother know to join us in the sitting room." She clapped her hands. "We have a wedding about to commence."

"That we do," Damian agreed as he entered the room. "One I've been waiting far too long for."

Pearla glanced at him with a sheepish smile. "Seems like we already had one wedding…not my fault it wasn't valid."

Damian chucked and hugged her tight in his embrace. He leaned down and kissed the top of her head. "That is true, but it is your fault for keeping me waiting for a wedding we both know *will* be valid."

Pearla held onto him and breathed in his scent. With him near, every one of her doubts and fears melted away. He always made her forget why she'd ever had a reason to object to being with him. She belonged in his arms. When they were wrapped up in each other, she couldn't help wondering why she fought him at every turn. He was right. They were inevitable.

"I know, and I can't apologize enough." She stepped back and gazed into his eyes. "I had these doubts and fears. I couldn't let them go. I've been let down too many times and didn't believe I could trust my own instincts with you."

"What changed your mind?" he asked.

"The truth?"

He nodded. She took a deep breath.

"No matter what I said or did, I couldn't get over you. You were always there at the back of my mind and when I saw you again…" She closed her eyes and took a deep breath. "I was so angry and betrayed. You left me when I needed you the most and had just begun to accept we could have something good. How could I not believe you would do it again? I had to protect my heart because no one has ever put me first."

His gaze softened. "Oh, *cara*…" He lifted his hand and caressed her cheek. "I didn't leave you. I was torn from you when all I wanted to do was stay with you forever. It was the worst thing that happened to me, and trust me, there have been some horrible things I've had to endure. Being away from you nearly devastated me. Knowing one day I'd be with you again gave me a reason to push on and fight."

Her insides turned to mush at his words. He may not have said the one word she hoped to hear, but how could he not love her when she gave him a reason to go on living? That was enough for now.

"Are you two ready to exchange your vows?" The vicar asked.

"Yes," they both said in unison.

The ceremony was fast and simple. They recited their vows, and before she knew it she was Damian's wife and the vicar announced that he could kiss the bride.

"My pleasure," Damian said and leaned down. Once his lips touched hers, sparks ignited into full-blown flames. Every time he touched her, she lit up with a need she couldn't describe. Only he had ever had that affect on her. He lifted his head and gazed down at her. She knew he had the same need pouring out of him by the color of his eyes. They always turned to molten silver when passion ruled him.

The vicar cleared his throat. "I guess I will be going now."

"Thank you again for coming on such a short notice," Noah said. "Let me see you out."

Damian looked up and watched them exit. "Rue, I think it's time that Pearla and I left as well." He hugged his sister. "Thank you for everything. We will come by again soon."

"You better." She laughed. "I've missed you. Besides you've yet to meet your nephew. Lucian needs to know his Uncle Damian."

He laughed. "I look forward to it."

Damian reached down and lifted her hand with his. He kissed the palm of her hand. "Are you ready to go home, *cara?*"

She frowned. "Where exactly is home now?"

He opened his mouth and then shut it again. "You're right. I have a bachelor residence."

A wide grin grew on Pearla's face. "The good news is I have a perfectly good townhouse. You can work on selling your rooms at the Albany tomorrow."

Damian laughed and escorted her out of the townhouse. "Do you have a carriage?" he asked.

"I do."

"Good. I walked over. I had a lot on my mind, and it gave me time to think." He kissed her lips. "Now I find I'm in a hurry to take you home."

Pearla smiled. "I am too."

They headed toward her carriage. She nodded at

the driver. When they reached the side, Damian leaned over to open the door—he crumpled to the ground before he could unfasten the latch. Pearla's gaze shot up. A man she'd hoped never to see again stood in front of her.

"Captain Blythe," she exclaimed. "What are you doing?"

"It's a pleasure to see you again, Miss Montgomery," he said. "I have to apologize for rudely interrupting your time with the conte, but I'm under orders to take you two to see my employer."

Pearla gulped down a lump that had become lodged in her throat. Who was he working for now? When he held her captive before, he'd worked for the Duca d'Sordillo. She'd been informed that the evil man was now dead. Who would wish her and Damian harm? As far as she knew they had no enemies to speak of. They were supposed to go home and bask in the glory of their finally being together. They were finally married, and their lives were once again thrown into tatters at the whim of a mad person.

"What if I don't cooperate?" she asked mulishly.

"If you'd rather I end Conte Leone's life now, I'd be happy to oblige." He shrugged. "Or you could come with me, and maybe you will both make it out of this alive."

"There's a chance we won't?"

A sick feeling settled down into the pit of her stomach. The dinner she'd consumed threatened to come back up. Why did these things continue to happen to her? She glanced down at Damian's unconscious body and made a snap decision. She couldn't take a risk with his life. He needed her to keep calm and make rational decisions. It was her turn to protect him and make sure nothing horrid happened to him again. If it meant going to meet the person who'd hired Captain Blythe, she'd do it. Then she would make them pay for interrupting her wedding night and threatening their lives.

She lifted her chin and said with conviction, "Take us to your leader. I have a few words they need to hear."

"Good girl." He laughed. "I knew you had some grit in you."

He gestured to someone behind her. They lifted Damian's body and tossed him in her carriage. Then Captain Blythe helped her inside. She sat next to her husband and caressed his hair. It comforted her more than it helped him. As the carriage rocked forward she formed a plan.

She was so done with insane people playing havoc with her life. It was time to let go of polite Pearla and let them feel the strength of her wrath.

First, she would have to make sure Damian was safe; although, she had no clue how she would be able to. Their fate didn't look good...

*a*n ache slid up his neck and traveled up to his head. A little hammer seemed to be beating a steady rhythm against it, causing pinpricks of pain to shoot behind his eyes. The idea of lifting his eyelids to check his surroundings didn't seem like a good idea. What the hell had happened to him? Last thing he remembered—Pearla.

His eyes flew open and he shuddered from the weight of them. Damian tried to sit up, but he couldn't move. He looked down and his hands were tied securely in front of him. His legs were secured to the sides of the chair he currently found himself in. There had to be a way to gain his freedom. His wife needed him. Who had hit him and taken him captive? This was starting to get old. He was on his way to his new home…to finally make love to Pearla.

"I see you're awake," a feminine voice filled his ears. He recognized it…where had he heard…

"Camellia," he replied scathingly. "Untie me, now." He jerked his legs and hands against the rope.

"Why would I do something as silly as that?" She sashayed over to his side. "I finally have you where I want you."

She was as crazy as her brother. How had he never seen it in her before? Was she as obsessed with him as Paolo had been with Rubina? Would he suffer a similar fate? Perhaps Camellia could be reasoned with.

"You have to know this is not a good idea. I will be missed."

She tilted her head and studied him. Her hair fell down her back in black waves. "I don't plan on keeping you here forever." She laughed. "I'm not my brother."

Damian stared at her, not saying a word.

"Oh, I see you are comparing us." She flicked her wrist nonchalantly. "I'm not crazy, Damian. Once were officially wed, you'll be free to go."

And she thought to convince him she hadn't lost her mind? Insanity clearly ran far and wide in the branches of that family tree. Reasoning with her might not work, but he still had to try.

"I can't marry you, Melia," he said softly. He really couldn't. He already had a wife.

"Sure you can." She smiled serenely. "The vicar will be here soon to perform the ceremony."

He hadn't really believed she was in the same league as her brother. Perhaps he should try reasoning with her again. It might help if he pled his case with her. She appeared rather calm about the entire situation. It scared him a little. It wasn't normal to hold the groom hostage before a wedding, and Camellia was acting like it was.

"You don't think he'll have issue with the groom being tied up for the ceremony?"

She strolled around the room and laughed. "Why would he?" She clapped her hands with manic happiness. "I've paid him well not to think at all."

He took a deep breath and studied her. There had to be a way to get through to her. She must care about him on some level if she wanted to marry him. Crazy, sure—but there must be a soft spot inside of her for him. He could try to play on that a little bit to get her to let him go.

"Melia," he coaxed. "I can't be your husband. It's the truth."

"Don't be ridiculous I told you already that you could."

He tried again, "I can't marry you because I'm already married to someone else."

Please don't ask who. He didn't know where Pearla was. He had to protect her, and he had no clue how far Camellia's insanity ran through her mind. She might get the notion to kill his wife so she could have him. What was it about his family attracting the mad people of the world? This one he could blame himself for. If he hadn't pursued Camellia for information on Paolo she might never have latched on to him.

She narrowed her eyes on him and glared. "Don't lie to me, Conte Leone. I won't be made a fool of."

He closed his eyes and prayed for patience. "I'm not lying."

"But…you love me," she said. "I know you do. The way you looked at me—it warmed me from the inside out. I was so sure…"

He shook his head. "I only love one woman, and I'm sorry, Melia." —He paused and looked into her stormy green eyes— "I owe you so many apologies for what I did to you. I used you in the worst possible way, but I never loved you."

She stalked toward him and leaned into him. Her

face mere inches from his and demanded, "Is it the blonde you were following around at the ball? Is she the woman you love?"

He gulped but held back from saying it.

"Never mind, I can see it in your eyes. You care for her." Her lips tilted into a half smile. "What was her name again? Pearla Montgomery if my memory serves me." She tapped her fingers together her smile growing bigger on her face as she stared at him. "You'll be happy to know I have her here. Captain Blythe is keeping her company while we prepare for our wedding."

Did she still believe they were going to get married? He'd already explained... She better not hurt Pearla. What would he do if she harmed his wife? There was nothing he wouldn't do for Pearla—even give his own life. "What are you going to do?"

"Wouldn't you like to know?" She strolled over to his side and raised her hand to cup his chin. She lifted her other hand and ran her fingers through his hair. "Don't you worry about a thing. I will make sure your wife is disposed of before the wedding."

She let go of his chin and took a few steps back. Damian jerked against the ropes, and they started to dig into his flesh with each attempt to free himself.

"Don't hurt her." He roared with frustration. "Please, I'm begging you."

Tears burned around the edges of his eyes, one escaping and trailing down his cheek. He'd fought so hard to get back to her. The hell he survived—it would be nothing without her. She was everything to him. If Camellia ended her life, she might as well take a dagger and stab him through the heart. He wouldn't be able to live without her.

Pearla had endured so much because of him. If not for the Fonte's obsession with his family, she'd be safe. She'd never have been kidnapped, either time. There was so much they hadn't discussed yet. He didn't deserve her love, but he wanted it. His self-ishness had brought this upon them. All he'd wanted to do was protect her. He'd failed. Now Pearla would pay for all his past mistakes.

"You really do love her, don't you?"

He glanced up at her. His vision was blurry from the tears threatening to flood his cheeks. "If she dies, do me a favor and kill me too."

"You poor, poor man." She smiled. "You're a besotted fool."

He blinked several times. "I have never loved a woman the way I do Pearla. She is my everything, always will be. If I don't have her, I have nothing. I would rather die than spend my life without her. So either kill me or let me go. If she's dead, I will find a way to leave this world on my own."

Camellia shook her head and laughed. "I never took you for the dramatic type. Relax, your wife is fine. I told you Captain Blythe was keeping her company. In fact, she's in the next room." She waved toward a nearby door. "She can hear everything we're saying."

His mouth opened and closed. Word failed to find their way out. "I don't understand."

What game was she playing now?

She sighed. "It was never my intention to hurt you, Damian. I thought I was doing you a favor."

"Tying me up and planning to marry me is your way of helping?"

He was oblivious to how her mind worked. Damian wasn't sure he wanted to know.

"Yes," she replied. "I was under the impression you were having difficulty getting Miss Montgomery to believe you really loved her. This was my way of alleviating every one of her doubts once and for all."

"What?" His vision blurred. "If you mean me no harm, then untie me."

"All in good time." She paced back and forth in

front of him. "Before I let you go, I need your assurance you won't hurt me." She shrugged. "There are also a few things I need to tell you."

"I won't hurt you." As long as Pearla was not harmed. "Loosen the ropes."

Camellia ignored him. "I have been searching for you for some time. I knew Paolo had done something to you." She sighed as she strolled around the room, and then stopped in front of him glancing down. She took a breath and continued her tone full of conviction. "I know how evil he is—was, and I wanted to make sure he hadn't done something irreparable to you. What he did to your sister was unforgivable. He wasn't any easier on me. He had me on a tight leash. His death freed me in so many ways. I owe your family a great debt."

"Untie. Me. Now."

"I will in a few moments," she replied. "I went to Bath because there was supposed to be someone with more information on how to find you. Captain Blythe wasn't being as forthcoming as I would have liked. I'd been informed Paolo had him do something to you. The captain refused to impart with the necessary information." She smiled. "Seems there are men worse than my brother. Can you believe that?" She raised an eyebrow, and then waved her hand dismissively. "He's said on several occasions he rather likes his head attached to his body. He's been most irritating. The blasted man has been following me in a misguided attempt to protect me. Imagine my relief to see you at that ball. I have been searching forever, and you seemed happy and contented with this little slip of a woman."

"She is more than that." Pearla was the only woman he'd ever love. If he managed to untangle them from their current mess, he'd make sure she knew how much he loved her. Camellia's insanity had taken a different direction than her brother's. Damian wasn't sure he appreciated her shaky moral code.

"I know she's the woman who captured your heart." She smiled at him. "I did some investigating and hatched this little plot of mine. I'm not crazy; I truly only want to see you happy, and I think I did help you. My methods might be a little...high-handed and a tiny bit extreme, but they are effective."

She snapped her fingers and the door opened. Pearla came rushing in with Captain Blythe fast on her heels.

"Oh, Damian, I'm so sorry. He wouldn't let me in until he got the signal from her." She glared at

Camellia. "Give me something to get these ropes off of him."

Captain Blythe shook his head and took several steps forward. He pulled a dagger out of a sheath and cut the ropes at his feet first. Then he slid it under the ropes around his wrists and cut them clean through. Damian rubbed his wrists and glared. How dare they put them through all the unnecessary torture? His fist connected with Captain Blythe's nose before he'd realized he had clenched his hand. The captain's bones cracked beneath his knuckles. It was by far the most satisfying act of violence he'd ever embarked upon. It would be gratifying if he could break more than his nose.

"Easy now," the captain said. "None of that is necessary."

"I beg to differ." Damian glared. "I've wanted to do that for too long now. You know you deserved it."

"You're both free to go," Camellia interjected. She turned her gaze toward Pearla. "I hope you can trust that he loves you now. There's no reason to doubt him."

Pearla nodded.

Damian stood and wrapped her in his arms. As stressful as it had been to wake up tied to a chair, he was relieved it had all been a farce on the part of Camellia.

"Camellia, if I don't see you for a long time—don't come looking for me." He glared. "Your way of helping doesn't work for me."

She laughed. "Conte, it's been a pleasure seeing you, but it's time for me to return to Naples. I have more messes of my brother's to clean up." She nodded toward Captain Blythe. "Are you coming?"

They both exited the room, leaving Damian and Pearla alone.

"I'm so sorry you had to go through that," Damian lifted his hands and cupped her cheeks. "I will spend the rest of my life making sure only joyful things fill your life."

"I'm sorry I ever doubted you."

"*Cara*, after all we have been through, I'd have been surprised if you hadn't." He loved her so much.

"Thank you for being patient with me." She leaned into him. "I love you too, even though I think I probably don't deserve you."

"I promise you, it's I who doesn't deserve you." He pressed his lips against hers. "I'm the lucky one. Before you, I only saw darkness. You are the light that gives me a reason to live and find pleasure in life."

"Why don't we agree that we are both blessed to have each other?" She hugged him closer. "Now take me home." She wiggled her eyebrows suggestively. "I believe you made me a promise or two you haven't fulfilled yet."

Damian chuckled. "We will work on rectifying those."

He wrapped her arm through his and led them out of the door. They had their whole lives together. Nothing but good things from now on—they'd already had enough excitement for two lifetimes. Damian was looking forward to easy going days and starting a family with his wife.

"I will say this much—this will be an interesting tale we can tell our children when they ask how we met."

Pearla laughed. "Once upon a time a man kidnapped us..."

"And we lived happily ever after."

Damian leaned down and kissed her, basking in the paradise of finding her love.

"Good morning, beautiful…"

Damian pulled her into his arms and trailed kisses down her neck. He dipped his head lower and ran his tongue across one of her breasts. He cupped the other one in the palm of his hand and pinched her nipple.

Need flooded through her. This is how every woman should wake up in the morning. Damian loved her thoroughly and left her breathless. Their desire for each other never wavered, even after being together for years and having three unruly children.

Pearla sighed as her body tingled with her husband's ministrations. "Damian, I need…"

"I know exactly what you need, *cara*." And he

proceeded to give it to her. He always kept his promises until she screamed from the pleasure of them.

This time was no different.

She basked in the glow of his loving. "I could lie here all day."

"Me too," he agreed. "Unfortunately, we must leave the warmth of our bed at some point."

Did they? Their bed was her favorite place, and when she was enclosed within his arms she didn't see any reason to leave it. Regrettably, they had responsibilities to see to outside of their bedroom.

Pearla sighed. "I know. I promised Gemma I would be down early to help her set up for the Viscount and Viscountess Torrington's surprise." She rolled out of bed and dressed. Damian languished behind and watched her. "Are you not going to come with me?"

"I was enjoying the view." He winked. "I will be down shortly. I have something I need to discuss with Noah and Liam."

She nodded and exited their room. They were at Huntly Manor, Noah's country estate. They were planning an intimate gathering to celebrate Liam and Lily's parents' anniversary. Forty years ago, they embarked on their own adventure together. Pearla hoped she would be as lucky as they were.

Their love had, thus far, stood the test of time. She and Damian had celebrated their fifteenth a few months ago. Their oldest child, Rafael, was born a year after they were married. Sofia and Gabrielle followed a few years after him, a year barely separating their births. All three of them kept her and Damian busy. They were full of life and too curious for their own good.

"Oh, good, I'm so glad you're here," Gemma exclaimed as Pearla walked into the sitting room. "I was afraid I'd have to come looking for you."

Pearla laughed. "I promised I'd help. What can I do?"

Four boys came running into the room. Liam and Gemma's twins, Alexander and Andrew headed the group. They were followed by Noah and Rubina's son, Lucian, and her own son.

"Mother, can you tell Angeline to quit following us everywhere we go?" Andrew demanded.

Gemma pinched the bridge of her nose. "Be nice to your sister."

Angeline was Gemma's youngest child, and her only daughter. She reminded Pearla of Lily. She took after her aunt a little too much. She was sure to drive

Gemma and Liam mad as she grew up. She fully understood Andrew and Alexander's frustration with their little sister.

"But..."

"No, Drew. You are her older brother. You should be used to having her follow you around. One day it will be your job to protect her."

"I told you." Alex folded his arms across his chest, glaring at his twin brother. "Next thing you know, Emilia will be joining her."

Emilia was Noah and Rubina's daughter. She was the spitting image of her mother. She had silvery blonde hair and beautiful gray eyes. Her beauty was going to cause Noah problems once suitors began clamoring for her attention. At least they had several years before they had to worry about it.

"I can assure you my sister has better taste." Lucian turned up his nose. "She would rather be a lady."

All four boys left the room, resigned to dealing with their younger sisters.

Pearla shook her head and laughed. Had they ever been that young? The years seemed to fly by, and before they knew it their children would be having families of their own. She wished she could bottle them up and keep them small forever.

"I'm sorry I'm late," Lily rushed into the room. "Brianne had a crisis with one of her dresses and was in a fit of tears. Sometimes I wonder how she could possibly be my daughter. If I hadn't given birth to her, I'd think someone was playing a trick on me."

Pearla glanced at Lily and laughed lightly. Her friend and been through a lot. They all had. After the birth of her son, William, Lily had been afraid she would never get pregnant again. She and Rand had tried to no avail. Pearla was so happy for them when they'd been blissfully surprised to be expecting again. Brianne was the blessing Lily never thought she'd receive. Although, she often remarked that her blessing was as opposite from her as she could get. Lily lamented often how her niece was more like her than her own daughter.

Gemma hugged her and laughed. "Where is she now?"

"She was trying to coerce William to play dolls with her. He tried to tell her he is a grown man now and doesn't play with dolls." Lily shook her head. "She's ten years old and doesn't understand why her big brother would rather do anything but play with her."

"She'll grow out of it, and he'll be an overprotective brother before long." Pearla turned toward Lily and asked, "Now that we're gathered tell me what we have left to do before your parents arrive?"

Lily was probably a general in a previous life. She barked orders and devised plans that would put some to shame. She lifted her hand and started checking off items on the list on her fingers. "Rubina is dealing with the menus and has the staff doing last minute decorations. Everyone that was invited, except my parents, is here. Noah and Liam arranged for them to arrive later this afternoon."

"It sounds like you have everything covered."

She grinned. "Planning has always been one of my strong suits."

"That's putting things mildly," her husband Rand said as he walked into the room. He pulled her into his arms and placed a quick kiss on her lips. "What do you need me to do?"

"Go rescue our son from Brianne. I'm afraid he might murder her if left with her too long."

He laughed. "Consider it done." He strolled out of the room, leaving the ladies to wrap up the festivities.

"Why did I get out of bed again?" Pearla asked. "I was rather warm and content there."

"I bet you were," Lily laughed. "Quit thinking of your husband and keep your mind on task."

"Why should I?" Pearla pouted. "You haven't given me anything to do."

They all enjoyed their husband's attentions. It was one of the things they discussed when they had nothing better to do. There were no blushes between them anymore. They were all well loved by the men in their lives.

"They're here," Rubina exclaimed as she rushed into the room. "They're early. I gave those two men one task and they seemed to have bungled it."

Pearla tilted her head and studied Rubina. She appeared to be stressed out about something. Who had arrived?

"No," Lily muttered. "Leave it to them to come early. I should have known they'd do something like this."

"Who's here?" Pearla asked.

She really should go back to bed. Her brain couldn't think past the pleasure of Damian's arms. It didn't seem as if they needed her help either way. Why not enjoy her day in other ways? The viscount and viscountess weren't supposed...she mentally groaned. How could she be so dense?

"I hear you're having a party for us," Thor bellowed as he entered the room. "When is it supposed to start?"

217

Pearla jumped from the boom of his voice. She'd met Viscount Torrington on several occasions. It was hard not to when she was so close to his children. He seemed sincere, but a small part of her remained terrified of him. He *had* been a pirate, after all. An endeavor that surely taught him how to give off a dangerous allure as natural as breathing.

Lily threw her arms up in the air. "I don't even know why I try. No one gets anything by him ever since I ran away and married Rand. Now he has spies watching us all the time."

"Princess, if I don't who will?" Lily's father kissed her forehead.

"You do have a valid point." Lily grinned up at her father.

Pia, Lily's mother, rolled her eyes. "Don't encourage him. He's already difficult to live with."

Thor, Viscount Torrington, glanced down at his wife; a hint of wickedness gleamed within his eyes. "You love every minute of it."

Pia, Lady Torrington, actually blushed from the heat of her husband's stare. Pearla didn't think it was possible to make the other woman's cheeks tinge with red.

"Grandfather, I thought I was your princess," a little girl asked as she tugged on his sleeve.

Rand followed behind her. He looked at Lily and shrugged, as if to say nothing could've stopped her. Brianne was a force to be reckoned with—much like her mother. That was the only thing they apparently had in common. Headstrong and determined to get their way.

Lily sighed. Pearla could relate. Her own daughters could be terrors on two feet.

"You're my other princess." He picked her up into his arms and hugged her. "Your mommy was the first princess to capture my heart. I think I have room for both of you."

"Will you play with me?" She pushed her bottom lip out. "William says he's too old to play with dolls."

"Did he?" her grandfather asked. "Don't worry I will have a talk with him later. Why don't you show me these dolls of yours? Are they as pretty as you are?"

"Of course not," she replied and pushed her chin out. "I'm much prettier. Daddy told me so."

Viscount Torrington glanced over at Brianne's father.

"Well she is," Rand replied.

Thor laughed and escorted his granddaughter out of the room. Pearla thought she heard him say, "This once I'll have to agree with your daddy. I didn't usually do it on principle." Pearla's heart melted watching them. She wished her own father had been this way with her. At least her children had Damian's father to dote on them. They didn't miss out the way she had growing up.

Damian, Noah, and Liam entered the room. Liam stared at his mother and shrugged. He too appeared to accept the inevitable and wasn't surprised to see his parents. Noah headed toward Rubina, and Liam joined Gemma. Damian strolled to her side and stood behind her, wrapping his arms around her. Pearla leaned into him and watched their friends and family. They were so blessed to have each other. As chaotic as their lives were, she wouldn't trade it for anything.

"Any regrets?" Damian asked.

It was a question he asked often. His way of checking to make sure she was happy with their life together. They didn't keep anything from each other. Their open communication was a gift they had received the hard way—at the hands of Camellia Fonte. One they never thanked her for, or intended to. It was a harsh way for them to begin to open up to each other fully. That night, after they made love for the first time, Damian finally told her everything that he endured on the island. She shuddered whenever she thought about what he had been through, but she kept his secrets close to her heart. If he wanted to share them, it was up to him. It was his past and his to keep to himself.

"Never." And she meant it. There was no reason to regret the choices they made. They had so many good memories already and many more they would make.

"I love you, *cara.*"

"I love you too."

Words that had become easier to say the more she uttered them. Her heart overflowed with happiness. Damian and their family was all she needed. The rest were just details. They could survive anything as long as they had each other. Damian would always hold her heart, and she trusted him to keep it safe always.

He kissed the top of her head. All her doubts were left in the past where they belonged. This was the life they were meant to have. One day their children would arrange such an event to celebrate their love and marriage. Their future was bright, and they had so much to look forward to. More importantly, they had all the blessings in the world to keep them content at that moment and for years to come. She'd once said nothing was forever. Now she knew better. Her luck had changed when she met Damian. It might have taken them a while to find their way to each other, but the struggle had only strengthened their bond.

Their love was all encompassing.

It was all she could ever ask for...

EXCERPT: REBELLIOUS ANGEL

MARSDEN DESCENDANTS ONE

DAWN BROWER

USA TODAY BESTSELLING AUTHOR

Dawn Brower

Rebellious
ANGEL

Christmas Wishes

CHAPTER 1

September 1906

The heat wave that rocked through the country had become unbearable. For Miss Angeline Marsden it heightened her anxiety levels. She had plans her parents wouldn't appreciate, but they would, in fact, give her hell about them. A girl had to stick to her beliefs, and Angeline had many. Some battles had to be fought the hard way, and others required a little more deviousness to come out the victor. Her parent's dislike of her cause required the latter.

If she had any chance of participating in the upcoming parade, she'd need help from someone close to her. More specifically, her best friend, Lady

Emilia St. John, and Angeline prayed she'd assist her. Otherwise, she didn't know how she'd manage to fool her parents. It had to work. This meant a lot to her, and she'd do just about anything to ensure it went her way.

Angeline rushed down the street toward the Huntly townhouse. Emilia was expecting her for afternoon tea. Hopefully Emilia's mother, the Duchess of Huntly, wouldn't be in residence. It might prove to be difficult to gain Emilia's assistance if they had to discuss it in whispers behind their silk fans. When she reached the door, she rapped on the knocker twice. A man with dark hair graying at the sides, opened it and greeted her, "Good day, Miss Angeline."

"Hello, Simmons." She nodded toward the aging butler. "Is Emilia in the sitting room?"

"Indeed, she is," he confirmed. "Her grace is as well."

Drat. She had hoped Emilia's mother would be out making calls instead. Normally, she'd love to visit with them both. She considered the duchess family of sorts. Her parents were close to Emilia's, and they'd grown up together. There were not many family gatherings that didn't include the Marsdens and the St. Johns. Unfortunately, though, her honorary Aunt Rubina wouldn't be any happier with Angeline's plans than her parents were. Somehow, she'd find a work-around. "Thanks, Simmons." She nodded at him. "I can find my own way there."

She didn't wait for the butler to respond. Huntly Manor had been a second home to her. Angeline was as acquainted with it as she was with the Marsden family estate. She went down the hallway and took a sharp right to enter the sitting room. It had been redecorated in dark blues and gold. The duchess had wanted a change, and the new color scheme gave the room a more elegant ambiance. A tea cart had already been delivered, and several cakes were displayed on a nearby table.

"Good afternoon," she greeted them.

The duchess wore a dark green walking dress decorated with gold buttons up the front. Her kid skin gloves matched it to perfection. She must have decided a hat was too much and had left her blonde hair unadorned. "Angeline," she said cheerfully. "It's so good of you to join us."

She smiled at the duchess. "It's been too long since we've seen each other." She leaned down and kissed her cheek. "How have you been?"

The duchess waved her hand. "You don't want to hear about our trip to the country. Noah had some estate business to handle, and I admit it was nice to rusticate at Huntly Castle. It's drafty and cooler then it is here. Can you believe this heat?"

Emilia rolled her eyes while her mother wasn't looking. The duchess would have chastised her for the unladylike behavior. Angeline repressed a laugh so she wouldn't get her friend in trouble. Emilia was a younger version of the duchess, down to the silver-gray eyes. She had even donned a similar shade of green as her mother—at times it could be disconcerting how alike they were. "Come sit." Emilia patted the cushion next to her. "Tell me what you're scheming these days."

Angeline stuck her tongue out. "I'm doing no such thing." Her friend knew her too well. There had to be a way to distract the duchess so she could find some time alone with Emilia. If she couldn't gain her assistance, her plan would be doomed. "I merely wished to visit my closest friend."

"That's lovely of you," the duchess said earnestly. "How are your mother and father?"

Hell bent on ruining my life... All right, the duchess wouldn't want to hear that from her—even if it was true. "They're both wonderful. Father was discussing the possibility of returning to the country estate. London really has become unbearable this past month. The heat is torturous." To prove that point, she flipped open her silk fan and started to wave it over her face.

"It's been a hard year for your family." Her voice held a hint of sadness to it. "With your grandfather..."

Angeline almost finished that sentence for her, but instead swallowed the lump in her throat. Her grandfather had passed away suddenly a year ago. Something that had hit her father hard—no one had ever expected the old man to die. Somehow, he had seemed so infallible. With her grandfather's unexpected passing, Angeline's father had become the next Viscount Torrington. A title he'd have gladly waited forever to claim if it had kept his father alive longer.

It was no secret that the former viscount had lived the life of a pirate before he'd married Angeline's grandmother. That had given him a dangerous aura that made any suitor interested in Angeline shake in fear. It didn't help that her own father could make a man freeze in place with one glance. Between the two men, she'd failed in securing a husband after several seasons. It was a good thing she didn't actually want a husband.

Well, that wasn't true either.

There was one man she wanted to marry, and unfortunately, he never paid any attention to her. But that was a problem she'd consider much later—maybe never. She would not let those old wounds dictate every decision she made. There were more pressing matters she had to focus on. Winning the heart of a clueless man was the least of her worries. "Grandfather will be missed," she reassured the duchess. "He'll never be forgotten. Thor was a stubborn, arrogant bastard, but we loved him—probably a little for those traits alone."

"That he did," a male said as he walked into the room.

Angeline's heart thumped inside her chest. She closed her eyes and took a deep breath, trying to calm the rapid thrusts of the traitorous organ. All he had to do was say one word and she wanted him. It had always been that way, and no matter what she did, it didn't change. Lucian St. John, the Marquess of Severn and heir to the Huntly dukedom and not to mention, he was also her closest friends' older brother and the one man she loved beyond reason.

His dark hair and chiseled cheekbones gave him a sinfully gorgeous face, but his silver eyes spoke of a devilishness she could only guess at. He had always been a perfect gentleman with her, but she knew he had a wicked side. Not personally... No, she'd never been so lucky as to taste passion of any sort. Rumors spread in abundance of how roguish he was, and she'd always been green with envy. She wanted him to look at her and desire her the same way she'd always longed for him.

"Hello, Mother," he said and leaned down to kiss the duchess's cheek. "I hope I'm not interrupting."

"Not at all dear," the duchess replied. "Are you here to join us for tea?"

"I wish I could," he replied smoothly. "I'm here to see Father, but I wanted to come say hello before we secluded ourselves in his office."

"Estate business?" His mother lifted questioning brow. "Never mind. I'm sure he'll tell me later. Are you sure you can't visit with us a little longer?"

As much as Angeline loved studying the man who held her heart without him noticing, she had other things on her mind. If Lucian stayed, that would make her goal even more difficult to achieve. Besides, it was slowly killing her to be around him. Nothing brought out the doldrums quite like his continued oblivion. She might as well be invisible when Lucian was around. He didn't bother to greet her unless good manners dictated he acknowledge her presence. Even now, he didn't turn his head and say the simplest of hellos to her or Emilia. He kept his attention focused on his mother.

"I must decline." His voice even appeared to hold a tinge of disappointment. Angeline doubted Lucian held an ounce of regret inside of him. Sure, he loved his mother, but he'd been decreed the wickedest of rogues. He probably would rather spend time in the company of a more delectable sort of female. Lucian was nothing if not smooth. "Perhaps we can have a family dinner later this week." Angeline swallowed the distaste in her mouth. Why had she gone and fallen in love with him? He'd never love her in return...

The duchess smiled, happiness radiating from her. "What a lovely idea." She turned to Emilia. "You can help me plan it, dear." Then she glanced back at Lucian. "We'll send a note to your townhouse when we decide upon a date. Go meet with your father. You know how he hates to be kept waiting."

"You're right," Lucian agreed. "Enjoy your tea." With those words, he left them alone in the sitting room.

Angeline couldn't help staring at him as he exited. Her gaze seemed to naturally follow after him whenever he was in the immediate vicinity. Would she ever put her feelings for him behind her?

She held back a sigh. It wouldn't help further her cause—any of them.

"Emilia," Angeline turned toward her. "It's such a lovely day. Do you care to go for a stroll with me?"

"Have you gone mad?" Emilia crinkled her eyebrows together. "It's as hot as the dickens outside." She flipped open her silk fan and waved it furiously over her flushed face. "I'd rather not exert myself any more than necessary."

This time Angeline did sigh. Emilia had a valid point, but she was running out of options. She wanted her help, so she'd have to figure out another way of discussing her problem with Emilia privately. "I'm...restless. I thought walking would help."

"Didn't you walk here, dear?" the duchess asked, her tone held a hint of skepticism to it. "I'd have thought that was more than enough exercise."

Her home wasn't far from Huntly Manor, so she didn't see any reason to have a carriage hitched for the short distance—even on a sweltering day. "If Emilia doesn't want to join me, that's her decision." Angeline had to hold back from reaching over and shaking her friend. She'd have to wait until the Wharton dinner later to find some alone time with her. "Perhaps I should skip tea and make my way home."

Her afternoon call hadn't gone as planned. She'd also had to suffer through time spent in Lucian's company—not that he'd acknowledged her. Maybe that was part of her problem. She'd longed for him since she was ten and two. Nine years later and her heart still skipped a beat whenever he neared.

"I didn't mean to imply you're not welcome," the duchess said. "Please don't feel as if you have to leave."

Angeline stood and went to the duchess to pull her into a hug. "You're gracious as always Aunt Ruby —it is as I said. I'm restless." She didn't want to make the duchess feel that she'd done anything wrong. It couldn't be further from the truth. If anyone could be held accountable for her agitation, it would be Lucian. She'd been on edge before she arrived at Huntly Manor, but his proximity made it even worse. Angeline stepped back. "Don't worry everything is fine, and I'll see you tonight at the Wharton dinner."

Emilia stood and wound her arm with Angeline's. "I'll see you out if you're so insistent on leaving before you've had any tea."

She scrunched up her nose. "It is hot out, and while I am parched, tea seems—too much right now." Truthfully, she'd lost her appetite—if she ever had one—the moment Lucian had stepped into the sitting room.

"It's never too hot for tea," Emilia replied. "Perhaps there's something else bothering you?" The corner of her mouth tilted upward into a sly smile. Her friend knew her to well…

They exited the room and walked down the hall leading to the foyer. Angeline didn't bother to comment on Emilia's not-so-subtle hint at Lucian's presence interrupting tea. "We'll have to talk more later. There's something I want to discuss with you."

"About Lucian?"

Angeline rolled her eyes. "Of course not. He's…" *Drat.* In a perfect world, he'd be her everything. Too bad Lucian would never reciprocate. "As much as I long for him to love me, he never will. You more than anyone know that. This is something more important."

"My brother is a fool," Emilia said and placed her hand on Angeline's. "We will talk more at the dinner. I'll help you with anything."

Emilia had always been there for her. Hopefully she was still willing to help once she realized what Angeline needed. She hugged her friend and left the manor. She had a lot to consider before the dinner later that night. Lucian could go to hell. He was probably the ruler of that fiery pit and the reason they were inundated with the unseasonably warm weather.

All right, he wasn't *that* bad... She wished he loved her though. However, no amount of hoping for the impossible would make it true.

ABOUT THE AUTHOR

USA TODAY Bestselling author, DAWN BROWER writes both historical and contemporary romance. There are always stories inside her head; she just never thought she could make them come to life. That creativity has finally found an outlet.

Growing up she was the only girl out of six children. She raised two boys into productive young men. There is never a dull moment in her life. Reading books is her favorite hobby and she loves all genres.

She is active on Facebook, Twitter, and Instagram. To follow her or can find more about her check out her website for the pertinent information:

www.authordawnbrower.com

bookbub.com/authors/dawn-brower
facebook.com/1DawnBrower
twitter.com/1DawnBrower
instagram.com/1DawnBrower
goodreads.com/dawnbrower

Broken Pearl

Deadly Benevolence

A Wallflower's Christmas Kiss

A Gypsy's Christmas Kiss

Snowflake Kisses

Diamonds Don't Cry

Kindred Lies

Begin Again

There You'll Be

Better as a Memory

Won't Let Go

Enduring Legacy

The Legacy's Origin

Charming Her Rogue

Scandal Meets Love

Love Only Me (Amanda Mariel)

Find Me Love (Dawn Brower)

If It's Love (Amanda Mariel)

Odds of Love (Dawn Brower)

Believe In Love (Amanda Mariel)

Chance of Love (Dawn Brower)

Love and Holly (Amanda Mariel)

Love and Mistletoe (Dawn Brower

Bluestockings Defying Rogues

When An Earl Turns Wicked

A Lady Hoyden's Secret

One Wicked Kiss

Earl In Trouble

All the Ladies Love Coventry

One Less Scandalous Earl

Confessions of a Hellion

Coming Soon

The Vixen in Red

Marsden Descendants

Rebellious Angel

Tempting An American Princess

How to Kiss a Debutante

Loving an America Spy

Scheming with My Duke

Secluded with My Hellion

Coming Soon

Secrets of My Beloved

Spying on My Scoundrel

Shocked by My Vixen

Heart's Intent

One Heart to Give

Unveiled Hearts

Heart of the Moment

Kiss My Heart Goodbye

Heart in Waiting

Broken Curses

The Enchanted Princess

The Bespelled Knight

The Magical Hunt

Ever Beloved

Forever My Earl

Always My Viscount

Infinitely My Marquess

EternallyMyDuke

Kismet Bay

Once Upon a Christmas

New Year Revelation

All Things Valentine

Luck At First Sight

Endless Summer Days

A Witch's Charm

All Out of Gratitude

Christmas Ever After

.

AFTERWORD

Thank you so much for taking the time to read my book.
Your opinion matters!
Please take a moment to review this book on your favorite review site and share your opinion with fellow readers.

www.authordawnbrower.com

ACKNOWLEDGMENTS

Thanks to all my readers for reading everything I write, and those that have been patiently waiting for me to finish writing the Marsden books. This is the final one, and I hope you love it.

Thank you to Victoria who has put up with me on the edits of these last two books. You have some amazing skills, and patience. These books are better because of your due diligence.

Finally thanks to Elizabeth, my original beta reader and amazing proofreader. You're awesome.

www.ingramcontent.com/pod-product-compliance
Lightning Source LLC
Chambersburg PA
CBHW030249200626
46816CB00002BA/571